*I wish I had seen the driver,
a license plate, anything.*

Her mind had been so locked on thoughts of Tyler that she'd been virtually oblivious to the traffic around her. When the oversized SUV had shoved her off the road, her car had rolled, coming to rest with the driver's side on the ground.

The tow truck driver had started strapping her smashed car down to his truck when Tyler's cruiser slid onto the scene, sirens blaring. He got out, then stopped when he saw the car.

Tyler put a hand over his mouth and rubbed it back and forth. He conferred with the supervising officer who turned and pointed at Dee.

Tyler followed his direction, and his gaze locked on her. His brows merged into one thick line as he scowled, and his eyes darkened to an intensity that made her sit up straighter. As he stalked toward her, her stomach tightened in a way that was part fear and part anticipation—she really wanted to avoid the coming confrontation, yet she truly felt relieved to see him.

Books by Ramona Richards

Love Inspired Suspense

A Murder Among Friends
The Face of Deceit
The Taking of Carly Bradford

RAMONA RICHARDS

A writer and editor since 1975, Ramona Richards has worked on staff with a number of publishers. Ramona has also freelanced with more than twenty magazine and book publishers and has won awards for both her fiction and nonfiction. She's written everything from sales training video scripts to book reviews, and her latest articles have appeared in *Today's Christian Woman, College Bound* and *Special Ed Today.* She sold a story about her daughter to *Chicken Soup for the Caregiver's Soul,* and *Secrets of Confidence,* a book of devotionals, is available from Barbour Publishing.

In 2004, the God Allows U-Turns Foundation, in conjunction with the Advanced Writers and Speakers Association (AWSA), chose Ramona for their "Strength of Choice" award, and in 2003, AWSA nominated Ramona for Best Fiction Editor of the Year. The Evangelical Press Association presented her with an award for reporting in 2003, and in 1989 she won the Bronze Award for Best Original Dramatic Screenplay at the Houston International Film Festival. A member of the American Christian Fiction Writers and the Romance Writers of America, she has five other novels complete or in development.

Ramona and her daughter live in a suburb of Nashville, Tennessee. She can be reached through her Web site, www.ramonarichards.com.

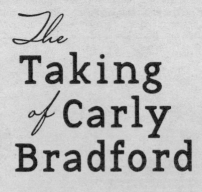

The Taking of Carly Bradford

Ramona RICHARDS

x

Steeple
Hill®

x

Published by Steeple Hill Books™

STEEPLE HILL BOOKS

Steeple
Hill®

Recycling programs
for this product may
not exist in your area.

ISBN-13: 978-0-373-44340-6
ISBN-10:   0-373-44340-4

THE TAKING OF CARLY BRADFORD

Copyright © 2009 by Ramona Richards

www.SteepleHill.com

Printed in U.S.A.

The Lord doth build up Jerusalem: He gathereth together the outcasts of Israel. He healeth the broken in heart, and bindeth up their wounds. He telleth the number of the stars; He calleth them all by their names. Great is our Lord, and of great power: His understanding is infinite.

—*Psalms* 147:2–5

It only takes one special teacher to change a life. My greatest fortune is that I had more than one. So this is for all the men and women who did what they could to share their love of learning and their wisdom… and to keep me out of trouble. I owe a huge debt of gratitude to all my teachers at Crestline Elementary, Pennington Elementary, Cameron Middle, Two Rivers High, Mt. Juliet High and the entire English department at Middle Tennessee State University.

So many thanks go to Mrs. Camp, Mrs. Kay, Mr. Dobbins, Mrs. O'Neill, Miss Hall and Mr. Waters, as well as others. And especially to Dr. Frank Ginanni, who seemed to truly believe I could make a living from my writing when no one else did.

Joshua was scared. He knew he was in trouble, but he didn't know what to do. "My parents will be so mad!" he told Rabbit. "They will never believe that my shoes walked away without me."

Rabbit looked back with sad eyes.

"You are right!" Joshua exclaimed. "I have to find them. Then, when my parents find me, everything will be all right."

—Dee Kelley
The Day My Shoes Took a Walk Without Me, 2003

ONE

"Drop the shoes!"

"No! Get away from me!" Dee Kelley screamed the five words, the sound tearing at her throat the way the trees around her tore at her body. Her face stung as a branch lashed her cheeks and forehead. The trees around her, the tips of their limbs vividly green with shiny new leaves, turned into a harsh field of obstacles as she fled, their boughs tugging at her clothes while their roots made every step uncertain. Dee risked a glance behind her, and she stumbled, going down sideways, her hip thudding into a patch of bright purple flowers in the undergrowth. A shriek burst from her lips as she twisted, fighting back to her feet, her right fist still desperately clinging to a pair of bright white children's sandals.

"Drop the shoes!" The rough voice sounded closer than before, almost at her back, and Dee could hear the running footsteps, the sounds of boots smashing into the soft, spring ground that had dogged her for almost half a mile.

A musty, sweet blended aroma of damp leaves and squashed flowers circled around her head as Dee demanded her exhausted body to rise off the woodland floor again. "Get up! Get up!"

This third fall had compounded the scrapes and bruises of the previous two. The winding and uneven path that traversed the two and a half miles from her writer's retreat cabin and the small, historic town of Mercer, New Hampshire, was familiar to her, but now she was far off the path, into the dense forest, running, gasping for air, hurting.

"What were you thinking?" Her hoarse words sounded flat as she struggled to her feet and ran, trying to ignore the voice behind her.

But she knew the answer as she grasped her aching side. She had been thinking that these white sandals could mean the difference between life and death. She just never dreamed it might be her own.

Tyler Madison picked up the picture of eight-year-old Carly Bradford that had remained propped against his desk calendar for the past three months. He examined yet again the delicate features and shining smile. Tyler thought all little girls were beautiful, but Carly's infectious grin and loving warmth drew everyone to her. Yet she remained completely and totally eight years old. Innocent and full of wonder. So he'd kept the picture there since that rain-soaked day when the petite princess had vanished to remind him of what really mattered.

As if he could ever forget.

An early spring rain had barely ended when Carly had dashed from her home wearing only a blue gingham dress, white sandals, and a yellow poncho to chase her puppy into the woods behind her home. The puppy had come home alone.

Tyler and his small force had exhausted all their resources on the foot-by-foot search of the area, to no avail. Carly had simply vanished, leaving behind no evidence of either accident or kidnapping.

He released a deep sigh, put the photo back on his calendar and pushed away from his desk. He recognized that finding Carly had become his obsession, but he didn't want to give up hope. It was not his nature to do so. After three months, however…

He stood, pacing his small office. He searched the Web every day for clues, but today he'd finished early. There was just nothing there. *Three months!* Everything had gone cold. The scant evidence, the interest of the community…even the press had been reluctant to keep her picture in their papers and on the Web sites unless something new turned up. The frustration of it gnawed at him, and Tyler knew he had messed up. What else explained it? Children didn't just disappear! They ran away, had accidents, were taken by relatives or strangers, but they didn't just vanish.

Tyler stopped. *OK, I have to focus on something else. Some other case or…something.* Jogging with his dog sometimes worked. Sometimes friends helped. He looked at the clock that hung next to his office window. Only ten o'clock, so he didn't even have the distraction of lunch with Dee and the other folks at the Federal Café. He grabbed his hat and checked his pocket for his keys. Maybe a drive would clear his mind, although he doubted it.

Somehow Tyler knew that the taking of Carly Bradford would haunt the rest of his life.

Dee smelled blood among the musky scents of earth and newly sprouted trees, and she knew it was her own.

Her face burned from the scratches and the salt of her sweat highlighted each wound with a sharp ache. Still, she pushed. She had to get to Mercer, had to find Tyler Madison. These shoes! She glanced at her fist briefly, her knuckles as white as the leather straps she clutched.

"Drop the sandals!"

Dee cried out, realizing the voice came from in front of her now, and she dodged to the left. She knew the road had to be just up ahead. Her mind grasped for a sliver of hope as she saw a break in the trees, there, farther into the woods, just to the left. Dee scrambled forward, reaching out for the next tree, then the next, her running shoes sinking deeper into the moist, moss-covered ground.

"Stupid woman! Drop them!" The voice sounded as if it were right behind her.

Dee could see the road now, the black pavement cutting through the forest like an ebony river. Safety. She had to get to...

A hand snagged the shoes, pulling her arm back and spinning her around.

"No!" Dee jerked them toward her, wrenching the sandals free from her pursuer. The figure behind her lost momentum with the action and stepped backward, grabbing wildly at a tree for balance. Dee got only a quick glimpse of the thin figure, face hidden behind a cap pulled low and a cloud of short dark hair, the frame indistinct in the black hooded sweat suit at least a size too big.

"You took Carly!" Dee screamed, her fear turning into a mother's rage. "Why would you do that?"

There was a quick shake of the head, then Dee's pursuer froze as a car whooshed by on the road up the bank behind Dee, as if for the first time realizing how close they were to traffic. Dee took advantage of the hesitation and turned, scrambling upward, her left hand digging into the dirt for traction. A hand clutched at her leg, but Dee jerked away, kicking backward. Her foot connected with flesh, and a sharp "oomph" echoed around her. But the action cost Dee her balance and she stumbled hard into a tree. She braced herself, then pushed away to go around it.

A branch hit her full in the face, as if it had been held back and released. A sharp pain shot through her nose, and Dee went down with a scream, one hand covering her face. Her eyes and cheeks stung as if she'd been slapped, and a hot stickiness covered her fingers.

There was another jerk on the sandals, and this time Dee screamed, an insane fury filling her. "No!" She swung her fist into a hard right cross, and the assailant went down, rolling back down the embankment.

Dee couldn't open her eyes wide enough to see anything. She screamed again as she fought her way toward the road, staggering on the rocky ground. *How could she be such an idiot?*

She knew she needed help. Just as she reached the pavement, unexpected drops of blood and sweat dripped from her brow into her left eye, blinding her. Dee tripped over the rough edge of the asphalt, right into the path of an oncoming car.

TWO

Light came back slowly. With it came the stark aromas of medicine and disinfectant, as well as someone's cologne. Dee could hear padded footsteps, the whispery sounds of low voices and the rustle of clothes near her bed. Behind her head, a machine softly beeped.

Hospital. I'm in the hospital. Where are the— She squinted and cleared her throat, grasping out with her right hand, which felt oddly empty. "The sandals…"

A soft pressure covered her wrist and the soothing baritone of Tyler Madison's voice attempted to comfort her. "Yes, we have the sandals. You gave them to me, remember? Dee. You need to rest. Just rest. Everything will be OK."

Dee struggled against the grogginess in her mind. "The shoes. Carly's shoes."

"Yes. You told me about them. Sleep."

The light faded a bit, as did the pain. The voices swirled around her in a fog, yet every moment in the woods remained as clear as luminous pearls on black velvet. Especially the moment she first saw the little girl's sandals. Carly's sandals.

The white leather had gleamed against the rich green

grass of the stream bank like a beacon, like the sudden appearance of a cherished memory on a bad day. The shoes were simple, just a wooden sole with white straps across the top of the foot. But they had a sweetness to them, as all little girls' shoes do, with the white leather straps etched with tiny stars. One shoe lay flat, while one rested on its side, but Dee Kelley knew they hadn't been on the stream bank long, since no splashes of mud dotted the leather.

Dee, however, knew she looked anything but perky when she had paused by the edge of the path to catch her breath, clutching a tree branch to stay upright. Her dark brown hair stuck in matted clumps to her neck, and sweat rivulets carved crevasses in her makeup. "Keep going!" Her voice croaked from lack of air and water.

Determination, however, had not stopped the cramp in her left calf, so she'd hobbled off the path to a shady spot at the edge of a stream. The stream ran beneath a narrow, wooden footbridge and extended several miles through the woods. She stretched her leg, gulping air and massaging the muscle. As the pain eased, she plopped down on the stream bank. "I hate exercise."

That's when she had spotted the sandals, their pale shapes standing out against the dark earth and grass of the stream's edge. "Someone must have gone wading."

Dee stood and placed one foot on a rock in the middle of the stream. She bent to lift the shoes out of the grass by their straps. As she straightened, she hesitated, puzzled. There were no other signs on the ground that a child had been anywhere near here. No footprints, no squashed grass, no rocks appeared tipped or out of place. Dee lifted the shoes and peered at them.

"So, did you walk upstream and just drop them, forgetting you had shoes in the first place?"

She smiled slightly, as a painful but beloved memory stabbed the back of her mind. Joshua had often done that, had constantly flipped off his shoes and gone without, forgetting where he'd left the dreadfully hot, confining things in the first place. Mickey had wanted to make Josh start paying for shoes out of his allowance, but Dee had resisted. *It's a kid thing. He'll grow out of it.*

Trying to soothe the issue between father and son, Dee had written a children's book, *The Day My Shoes Took a Walk Without Me,* told from Joshua's point of view.

Dee took a deep breath and pushed the memory away. Part of her ongoing plan for recovery meant allowing the memories in but not dwelling on them. After all, dwelling on the past had kept her locked in her parents' house for almost three years.

"Keep moving," Dee said aloud, as much about her exercise as her past. The sandals still dangling from her fingers, Dee struggled back up the bank to the path. Stretching again, she continued toward her goal at a fast walk, reluctant to break back into the jog that had caused the cramp in the first place.

Her goal was the Federal Café, in downtown Mercer. Those three years of seclusion had added some extra weight to her petite frame, and Dee had become determined to rid herself of it. So, every day she walked or jogged the path into Mercer for a sensible, low-calorie lunch at the café with her new friends. She then took the road that ran from Mercer through several neighborhoods and the wooded area back to the retreat.

Dee picked up her pace a bit, the sandals bumping against her leg with almost every swing of her arm. Her mind drifted to the way she looked in a size eight. In particular, an emerald green dress that Mickey had given her just a week before the accident....

Dee stopped and lifted the sandals again, peering at them. Something about a pair of children's sandals tickled the back of her brain, and she let it drift there for a moment. There was something...in the news... sandals, wooden soles and straps with stars on them....

The wind sucked out of Dee as if she'd been punched, and her knees buckled. She sat down hard on the ground. Carly Bradford! These had to be Carly's. A sudden panic flooded over her. "What do I do—?"

Tyler. She had to get to Tyler. He would know what to do. He was always at the café this time of day; they usually ate lunch together. She picked up her pace, then broke into a jog. She had to get to the—

"Drop the shoes!"

The voice, harsh and low, came from Dee's right, and she stumbled, almost falling into a bush. She spun, listening, unsure if she'd really heard a voice or if her mind had turned the rustling of squirrels and birds into words.

"Drop the shoes!"

Dee had instead turned and fled.

Tyler leaned against the wall in the examining room, watching Dee breathe, every muscle tightening when she shifted restlessly on the bed. The bruise around her left eye had grown to the size of his palm, framing a network of scratches on Dee's swollen, misshapen face. Tiny butterfly bandages held several of the cuts closed, including one across the bridge of her nose.

His mind reeled to think how close he had come to killing her. He'd almost panicked when she'd darted into the road, and precious minutes passed before he realized that, although his fender had grazed her, most of her injuries were from an attack in the woods.

He'd bundled her into the car and headed for Portsmouth at lightning speed. He had radioed the station to alert the hospital and sent Wayne Vouros, his sole detective and crime scene specialist, to the site of the attack. He'd also called Fletcher and Maggie MacAllister, owners of the writer's retreat where Dee lived. Maggie was a close friend of Dee's, and she now waited impatiently outside the E.R. while Fletcher had joined Wayne at the scene, promising to call as soon as they knew anything.

Tyler shifted his weight and checked his cell phone one more time, even though it had not vibrated since he'd arrived at the hospital. He replaced the phone, then took a deep breath to quiet his increasing anxiety, his need to *do* something.

Finally, he gave in to the gentle urgings of one of the nurses and sat in a hard plastic chair near the bed. He leaned forward, elbows on knees, and clutched his hat in one hand. He examined the band closely, for no good reason. He just needed somewhere to look that wasn't Dee—or the smears of Dee's blood that still streaked his clothes.

How could he have been so blind? Tyler knew that deer leapt out on that stretch of road all the time, yet he'd trundled through, his mind so on Carly that he had become oblivious to everything else.

Lord, I could have killed Dee. Please let me be more alert and aware.

Not that he was normally unaware of Dee. In fact, he'd been increasingly aware of her since she'd arrived in Mercer, with her sharp wit and soft Southern accent. He looked forward to their lunchtime meetings at the café, her questions about Mercer's residents and history, her thoughts about life in the South.

Tyler rotated his hat in his hands. He enjoyed the way she looked, too, despite the weight she said she wanted to lose. He didn't get that, the weight loss thing, even though he could stand to lose a few pounds, as well. He liked Dee's curves, the way her dark hair caressed her shoulders with the soft curls at the tips. She barely came up to his shoulder, so she was maybe five-two, but she seemed just right to him.

What is taking so long? He glanced at his still silent phone again. Never had he so badly wanted to be in two places at once, to see how she was doing here, but also at the scene of her attack. *Maybe I should let Maggie take over here.* Then he immediately dismissed the thought. Wayne and Fletcher were certainly capable of handling the gathering of any evidence, whereas Maggie had no training with crime victims. He needed to be here when Dee awoke, not Maggie.

He paused. Interesting friends, those two, the New Yorker who had adopted Mercer as her home and the Southerner who had seemed so lost a few months ago. Maggie had been tough on Dee at first; now they were friends. Maggie could be surprisingly hard on the writers at the retreat, even though she was younger than most, maybe thirty-one or so.

Hmm. How old was Dee? Tyler shifted in the hard chair, trying to find any kind of comfortable position, as he attempted to do the math of Dee's life. He looked again at her face, so oddly relaxed now under the criss-crossing bandages. He knew she'd been married for about ten years, and that her son had been eight when he died three years ago. That would make her, what, early to mid-thirties? She still moved like a younger woman, though...

He stood, pulling his phone out again, as if the ring tone had stopped working for some reason. Still nothing. He glanced at the clock again. *Stop getting distracted.*

He paced slowly, quietly. There had been too many distractions lately. *Focus on the case. What if Dee's mumblings about the sandals were right? Were the sandals yet one more thing they had overlooked?* He knew without a doubt they had searched that stream bank. With a child Carly's age, the stream always got checked first.

Yet all previous cases of missing children in Mercer had been about runaways, all of whom had returned home quickly. In his ten years on the force, nothing like this had happened. A true kidnapping. And although he'd gained a lot of confidence and experience in the four years since he'd become chief, Mercer did not lend itself to giving him experience in major crimes. Robberies, assaults, an arson or two, the occasional domestic dispute—these were routine. But since the town had separated itself from the county and organized its own law enforcement department apart from the county sheriff's team, the police had handled only one murder and no other major crime.

Tyler's mouth twisted grimly, and he dropped back down in the chair. Of course, Mercer's low crime rate gave him plenty of time to obsess about a missing little girl. The very idea of someone swiping a kid filled Tyler with a stomach-churning revulsion. He couldn't imagine why anyone would be cruel to a child, and he knew most kids were found within a day or so—or not at all. Whether or not they were found depended a lot on the initial investigation.

The initial investigation. Tyler felt out of his league and terrified of making another misstep. He had made plenty in this case, even with the FBI and the state police helping and his best friend, former NYPD detective Fletcher MacAllister, looking over his shoulder. An Amber alert had not been issued due to the lack of evidence that Carly was in immediate danger; no proof existed that she'd been taken as opposed to running away. He had told Carly's parents—and the media—too much about their investigation. The lack of evidence had panicked him into asking the wrong questions of the wrong people, leading to a lot of misinformation in the press, and the Bradfords were even more devastated by the publicity. Every day the case had grown colder as early spring rains washed away the last semblance of evidence. There were, in fact, no leads at all, and even now no evidence that she'd been kidnapped. Not even a clean indication of a crime scene.

Yet everyone in Mercer knew that the happy princess had not run away. Tyler ached to prove it. To find her.

He shifted in the chair. *Stop whining. Focus on the facts. What few there are.*

The Bradfords had no known enemies. Jack and Nancy Bradford were beloved members of the community with no apparent enemies. Even though Jack was a Portsmouth surgeon, he'd been out of medical school only a few years. He'd never been sued and only had one complaint against him registered with the American Medical Association—and the AMA had cleared him in that case. Nancy had given birth to Carly when she and Jack were still in college, barely making ends meet. They were a family made close by hardship, and they adored each other. Almost no one Tyler interviewed had a bad word to say about them.

Carly often played in the woods, but at no set time. The only conclusion anyone could draw was that it had been a random act, a moment of opportunity. A cruel stranger who had happened to see the lovely child skipping along after her dog and decided to…

"Tyler?" The voice came from behind him, and he turned. The young woman who stood there—tall, blond and exceptionally thin—could have been mistaken for a model, except for the white coat and the perpetually exhausted look of an E.R. physician. As police chief of a small town without a hospital, Tyler knew all the E.R. docs in Portsmouth and Manchester. "Hello, Anna," he said quietly.

Her warm smile was genuine but looked as tired as her eyes. "Hi, Tyler. She one of your Mercer folks?"

"Yes. And a friend."

Anna nodded. "Then you might want to keep an eye on her for a few days." She slipped her hands into her jacket pockets and her doctor mode took over. "She took quite a blow across the face. She says it was from a tree branch, and I don't doubt that. No sign of concussion, though, which is good news. As you can see, we've stitched up the cuts and given her something for the pain."

"Pain." Tyler took a deep breath. "Will she be coherent if I talked to her about what happened?"

Anna paused, focusing on his eyes, considering the question. After a moment, she glanced at Dee, then shook her head. "She has a lot of meds in her now, but she's asleep, not unconscious. She should stir soon, but she'll still be loopy. She didn't make a whole lot of sense before the meds, but now, you may not be able to tell when it's Dee talking and when it's the drugs doing the speaking. She needs to rest for a day or so, but she'll be okay and far more able to tell you her story tomorrow. The nurse is prepping the release paperwork, so they'll bring her out in a few minutes. Mostly, she needs quiet."

Tyler nodded. "Thanks. We appreciate your help."

Anna paused, then put a hand on his forearm. "If she needs me, page me. I'll meet you here."

He wrapped his fingers briefly around hers, then she returned to her work.

When Tyler returned from the treatment area, Maggie stood immediately. "How is she?"

Tyler held up the two plastic bags the hospital had loaned him, one holding a pair of white sandals, the other the contents of Dee's pockets. "Shook up. Her face is all scratched up, and her left eye is black and swollen shut. Her doctor thought she'd broken her nose, but it's just badly bruised."

She looked up at Tyler, then pointed at the bag with the sandals. "What are those?"

He motioned for her to sit, then dropped into a chair next to her. "She kept mumbling about these all the way here. I couldn't even get her to let go of them. She kept repeating that she'd heard a voice in the woods, demanding that she drop the sandals. She ran, but the voice chased her." He paused, watching her closely. "She says they're Carly's."

Maggie fell back in the chair as if she'd been punched, and her voice became a tight, hushed whisper. "Carly's? How could they be Carly's?"

He shrugged. "She said she found them by the stream."

Maggie straightened. "That's impossible. We searched every inch of that stream bank, the entire run of it. The whole town did."

"I know."

She shook her head. "And we've had other false finds. They can't be Carly's."

"I know."

"It's almost too weird to believe." She paused. "If I didn't know Dee, I'd think she was..." Her voice trailed off, and she seemed to sag a little.

"Hallucinating?" Tyler asked.

Reluctantly, Maggie nodded.

"Except she didn't smack herself in the face."

They fell silent a moment, then Maggie pointed at the other bag. "What's in that one?"

"The stuff from her pockets." He turned the bag so they both could see the contents: a cell phone, keys, a pack of mints and a Swiss Army knife. He frowned at them. "She carries a Swiss Army knife?"

"Everywhere she goes. I think it belonged to her husband. Dee isn't crazy about carrying a purse." Maggie looked down at the floor a second, then back up at him. Squaring her shoulders, she stood. "What if she's right? What if these are Carly's and someone did attack Dee? What then?"

Tyler rose as well, watching her face closely, trying

to read her meaning. Was this about Dee? Or the fact that those woods bordered the retreat's property? Fletcher had once told Tyler that Maggie seemed to adopt all the writers at the colony, taking them under her wing no matter what their age. Encouraging, sympathetic, and patient with the creative egos, Maggie became their sister, mother, or daughter, depending on their needs. He also knew that Dee held a special place in Maggie's heart. Tyler saw that in her now, the light of deep compassion in her hazel eyes.

He took her hand in his. "Then we'll protect her. We'll get her story and investigate. We'll call the FBI and ask for their help again. We'll have to revisit a lot of what we've done on Carly's case."

Maggie breathed deeply, her voice barely above a whisper. "If they are…I mean…would this mean she could still be in the area? Does this mean that Carly is still alive?"

THREE

Somewhere over her head a door slammed violently, and a scream of pure fury echoed throughout the house. Carly Bradford whirled away from the narrow window of the basement room and dropped back down on the bed beneath it. She scooted close to the headboard and drew her knees up close to her chest, waiting, her eyes locked on the overhead vent that allowed in cool air and a lot of noise from upstairs. She followed the booted footsteps as they crossed the ceiling, then thudded down the stairs into the basement and across the short passage outside her door. There was an odd sound of rustling metal that she could never quite figure out, then keys rattled, the lock scraped and the door swung open.

Her captor entered, face red with anger, and Carly knew immediately that the sandals had not been found.

"I'm sorry. I didn't mean to drop them…" She stopped, and Carly's eyes widened as she took in the bruised face and the streaks of mud on the legs and chest of the sweat suit her captor always wore into the woods. Something had happened.

Carly flinched, a new wave of fear surging through

her, and she hugged her legs tighter. "Please don't hit me again."

"Someone took them. I tried to stop her—" Her captor waved a hand in dismissal. "Never mind. I want the dress."

Carly pointed, hand trembling, to a trunk in the corner. "It's still there."

Shortly after her captor had locked Carly in this tiny bedroom, new clothes had appeared on the bed, with orders to put the sandals, poncho and dress into the trunk. There they had stayed until last night, when her captor had awakened Carly well after midnight and announced that she needed exercise. Her captor had not bought new shoes for her, so they had retrieved the sandals. They had walked the stream bank into the woods, following only the light of a full moon. Her captor had tried to make her laugh and play, as if all were normal, despite the rope tied securely around Carly's waist and a hushed threat of what would happen if she screamed. Exhausted, terrified, Carly had tried, finally slipping off the sandals and wading downstream a bit, then back. Only after they had returned home did they realize the sandals were gone.

Her captor snatched the blue sundress out of the box and waved it at the young child. "I'll get them back. Have to. No matter what it takes. That meddling witch…" The dress snapped like a flag in the wind. "If this doesn't work, we'll have to move." The door slammed, and the lock clicked back into place.

Tears leaked from Carly's eyes as the frightened, confused little girl rolled over on the bed. "I want to go home." The pillow muffled her words and soaked up her tears, but she grew quiet as something her captor had said echoed again in her head.

Someone took them...her...

Someone. A woman. Maybe the rescuer Carly had been praying so feverishly for? Carly looked up at the ceiling. "God? Can she help?"

Is Carly still alive? Maggie's question haunted Tyler all the way back to Mercer, just as it had clung to almost every waking moment for the past few weeks. He drove back alone in his cruiser, with Maggie insisting that Dee ride in her larger and more comfortable SUV. Anna had been right. When they brought Dee into the waiting area after her discharge, the medications had completely clouded her mind. Incoherent and groggy, Dee had almost fallen out of the wheelchair, and Tyler's chest tightened as he looked over her injuries and tried not to show his surprise.

Tenderly, he'd lifted her from the chair and snuggled her down into the backseat where Maggie had made a nest of coats and blankets borrowed from the hospital. "Ride easy, Dixie Dee." He had whispered it so softly no one else could hear, and she'd blinked up at him, then closed her eyes sleepily as he'd tucked a pillow in at her side.

He'd backed away as Maggie took over as nurse, and Tyler returned to his car with the bag holding the sandals. As both cars pulled out of the hospital's parking lot, he called Fletcher. "Speak to me. Where are you?"

The older detective cleared his throat. "Just leaving the scene. It's getting too dark to do any more tonight. How's Dee?"

Tyler related what Anna had told him about the attack and Dee's condition. "Anything to corroborate her story?"

"Some. Wayne found blood spatter around a tree, and drops leading to the road near where you hit her. He also found blood and bits of skin on one of the limbs. There are at least two sets of footprints, one most likely Dee's, but we couldn't tell if there were more than two. The ground is badly torn up. We took a couple of casts, just in case. Wayne gathered some of the blood and skin to send to the lab, but my guess is that it's all Dee's."

"Hear any spooky voices out in the woods?"

Fletcher paused. "You don't believe her?"

Now it was Tyler's turn to hesitate. "I don't know, Fletcher. Her injuries are real, and it does sound as if she had a scuffle with someone. I don't think she made this up. I just don't know if she heard what she thinks she heard. It could have been a kid trying to scare her. What's your take on this?"

Another pause. "The wind in these trees can sound strange to anyone not used to it."

Tyler grinned. "So says the boy from New York City?"

"Not me," Fletcher growled. "I grew up in Vermont."

"Right." Tyler let him off the hook. "Listen, Maggie is taking Dee to the retreat lodge house. She'll play nurse, but if you could…"

"Not a problem. And I'll keep an eye out."

"I know Dee will remember things differently tomorrow, but there was no way to get a statement out of her today."

"Assault victims usually do."

"Is Wayne going to send everything to the lab?"

"Yeah. He said to tell you to go on home. The boys are changing shifts, and he'll take care of the rest of this. You can do any remaining paperwork in the morning."

"I'll drop the sandals off so he can log them in and put them in a proper evidence bag. If, in fact, they *are* evidence, I don't want to leave them in the car overnight nor in a plastic bag."

"You know you'll have to call Jack and Nancy about this before you do any forensic work on them."

"I know. Can't spend the money on forensics unless we know for sure. We've already been through this too many times."

A beat of silence passed before Fletcher spoke again. "You want me there?"

Absolutely! You think I want to do this by myself once again? Look into those faces, offer them some kind of false hope again? "No. Thanks, though. I need to do it."

"If you change your mind, let me know."

Tyler hung up, following in silence as the cars turned into the long drive leading to Jackson's Retreat. He carried Dee from the car into a guest bedroom in the retreat's lodge house, then stood back awkwardly as Maggie took on the role of Dee's caregiver. Normally the writers stayed in individual cabins on the property, but this way Dee would be close to Maggie and Fletcher, who would guard her as if she were a queen.

Maggie still bustled about the virtually unconscious Dee as he eased out of the room and returned to his cruiser. The ten-minute drive to the police station felt much longer, with his mind occupied by the innocent eyes of Carly Bradford and the wounded face of Dee Kelley. He gave the sandals to Wayne to log in for evidence, then headed home.

An odd sense of resignation settled around Tyler as he drove to his small house not far from downtown and let go of any idea that the sandals belonged to Carly. They couldn't. That style had been quite popular for young girls this spring, and they had already received a dozen or more false "sightings" of the shoes. This was just one more. But, of all the people to find another pair of "Carly's shoes," did it have to be Dee Kelley, with her wounded mother's soul? He couldn't imagine what was going through her mind and heart right now.

Help her, Lord. Tyler's silent prayer came automatically to him. *She's already been through way too much.*

He also hoped that this "attack" was more than Dee's imagination, that it didn't mean Dee was about to spiral viciously backward into her old life. *She's come so far since being here, Father. Don't let her go backward in her healing. She's going to need Your help.*

Everyone in Mercer seemed to know Dee's heart-crushing story, of how she'd lost her husband and son in a devastating car crash and the three-year depression that followed. He'd heard different versions from a variety of townspeople, including Laurie at the café and a couple of shop owners. As usual, small towns and personal secrets weren't a good mix. Yet knowing it had led the locals to embrace this newcomer in a way they seldom did. Of course, it helped that they'd discovered Dee to be one of the most gracious people they'd ever met.

He sighed as he turned on to his street, his mind flipping back to the day he'd met her, not long after she'd arrived in Mercer. Tyler and Fletcher had grown close over the past couple of years, and he often ate dinner with the MacAllisters and the writers at the retreat. One day, a few months ago, Dee had joined them. She'd been polite but reserved, and had spent most of the meal watching birds whisk to and fro at the feeders on the back deck of the lodge.

Tyler, on the other hand, spent the time watching her, drawn in even more when Fletcher had recounted her full story to him later that evening. The two of them had retreated to the basement game room of the lodge with hot cups of coffee to discuss cases and long days on the job. Then, when Tyler's increasingly curious questions about the new writer started to amuse Fletcher, he switched the subject to Dee. Fletcher's tale captured both Tyler's imagination…and a bit of his heart.

Fletcher explained that Dee had seldom left her small Southern town before the accident. "She did, however, spend a lot of time on the Internet, which is where she met Aaron." Aaron Jackson, a best-selling novelist, had started Jackson's Retreat as his literary legacy, and he'd sung its praises to Dee when they had met during a writers' conference. An immediate connection had sprung up between them, and they found a lasting friendship in their common beliefs. Aaron and Dee had e-mailed almost every day, sharing stories and problems.

Aaron had also been one of the few out-of-town friends to come to the funeral of her husband and son three years ago, following the car accident that had destroyed Dee's world. Aaron had even remained several days afterward, holding her and letting her sob and rage at someone other than her parents and God.

Aaron's murder a year later had been the last straw for Dee's already fragile mind, and she had descended into a darkness she thought endless. A darkness completely devoid of hope, faith, and love. Devoid of God.

Her mother, however, remembered Aaron's retreat

and found some of the correspondence on Dee's computer. Her parents, conspiring with Maggie, had put Dee on a plane.

Tyler had scowled at Fletcher. "Why am I just meeting her now?"

Fletcher sipped his coffee. "Because she's just now emerging from her cabin. She's not done much except stare at the walls."

The first month at the retreat had been more darkness, with Dee lying for hours on the bed in her cabin. Maggie, with a new baby on her hip, had gone to the cabin every morning, opened the blinds and windows, turned on the lights and ceiling fan, and booted up Dee's computer. Maggie had returned in the evening with Fletcher to insist Dee join the group for dinner. Dee had initially refused, and Fletcher and Maggie had stayed with her, eating dinner in her cabin and forcing her to talk to them. They learned the more intimate details of Dee's life, during those first days, when Dee began to share her words with them, long before she started coming to the lodge for dinner.

Slow therapy, but it worked. Listening to other writers around the large dining table had finally engaged Dee in challenging conversation, and, eventually, had inspired her to sit at the computer, if only to stare at the blank screen. Six weeks later, she started to write. A journal, at first, then essays, two of which she sold to parents' magazines. Those first paychecks buoyed her in a way she had not expected, letting a tiny glimmer of hope into her mind and heart. Tyler had met her as that glimmer of hope had begun to grow. Yet, the one thing still missing in her life was God. She had not reopened her heart to Him at all.

The bump that edged the entrance to his drive yanked Tyler back to the present, and he now prayed silently that God would make sure Dee held on to that hope. "She needs You more than ever, Lord, even if she doesn't think she does," he whispered, as he pulled into the drive at the side of the house and let the car roll to a halt in front of a garage near the back of the property.

Well, it was supposed to be a garage, but the building had never held a car as long as Tyler could remember. The previous owner had been on his way to an assisted living facility when he sold the house, and had left the garage stuffed with all the yard tools Tyler would ever need, plus some he didn't even recognize.

The owner also left Tyler a dog, which now stood peering at him from the back porch, her front half outside the pet door, looking calm. The back half, however, gyrated so violently that the pet door bounced up and down on her back. Patty, a supremely obedient peekapoo named for the New England Patriots' mascot, always waited for permission to welcome him home, but she jiggled, wagged, and whimpered until she seemed ready to split apart at the seams if he didn't give it.

Tyler couldn't help but grin. He got out of the car, and Patty's increased excitement made the entire back door vibrate in its frame. He clucked his tongue and patted his thigh, and Patty launched herself off the porch, propelled by healthy muscles and pure love. When she got close, she bounced up on her hind legs, dancing a bit until he scratched her under the chin and praised her, their welcome-home routine. Then she whimpered with pleasure and pressed herself up against his leg briefly before prancing alongside him as he entered the house.

Tyler paused and let out a deep sigh as he closed the door and removed his gun and holster and placed them in a cabinet near the door. Home. It felt good. He'd waited so long to buy his own place that some folks thought he never would. But Tyler wanted just the right house, and he was patient. This former residence of a retired teacher and confirmed bachelor had been just the right house. Well-kept and already decorated in the dark greens, blues and browns that Tyler found comforting. He'd changed very little in the house, but it was still *his* space.

I wonder if Dee would like it. Images of the short brunette slipped in and out of Tyler's mind as he prepared dinner—a scoop of dry food for Patty and a sandwich and chips for himself—then cleaned the kitchen and stretched out to watch one of the news channels for a bit. He liked Dee's laugh, and he thought again of their great chats over lunch at the Federal Café. He found her questions about his life and his faith intelligent and curious without being intrusive. He'd encouraged her to look to God again, trying to give examples of perseverance and success from his own life as well as his friends'. She still resisted, even if her curiosity about his own faith never waned. Maybe, as she healed from her grief.... He sighed. "Special lady."

Patty, who had parked herself by the couch within reach of his petting hand, perked up at his muttered words, tilting her head to one side, as if to ask, "Did you say 'walk'?" She twisted in the other direction.

Tyler scratched her head. "Let me change, and we'll go out. Maybe this will clear my head."

Patty bounded up and over to the row of pegs behind the back door where her leash hung. He laughed, then went upstairs to the bedroom to change into shorts and a long-sleeved T-shirt. By the time he had his running shoes on, Patty had turned into a wriggling maniac, and he calmed her down, then snapped on the leash.

They started out with a slow walk, with Patty darting around him, sniffing every post, mailbox or clump of grass that hinted of a previous dog's passing. They circled the block near his house, and he waved to any neighbors out for late evening chores or porch sits. Mrs. Adams, eighty-three and still a pistol, flagged him down to complain about a stray dog that had been digging in her yard. Tyler promised he'd speak to the county's animal control folks and complimented her on her beds of spring flowers. The Beekers, transplants from Boston, asked about the spring arts festival, and he referred them to the gallery owner who organized it.

Eventually, he and Patty headed toward the city park at the edge of town. Dusk gave way to a pleasant darkness, with the moon already rising, turning open areas silver as the shadows became more stark and defined. The park had a graceful, steady slope to it, and many of its features—the bandstand, memorial fountain, and the cluster of benches that was his favorite prayer spot—faced Mercer, so that everything appeared to overlook the small vale where the town sat so peacefully.

Tyler jogged around the perimeter of the park once, checking out anything that might look suspicious, then circled it again in a fast jog. The last of the visitors—a couple he knew from church and a scattering of young boys squeezing as much out of the day as possible—wandered toward the park entrance. At the end of the second trip, the jog turned back into a walk, and he and Patty headed home.

He'd once clocked it at 4.6 miles, and Tyler claimed every foot. He didn't like to run; he did it because he needed to stay in reasonable shape for the job. Having Patty along made it palatable, and he'd gotten asked out recently because of the dog. He grinned. Maybe he should introduce Dee to Patty.

Yet as he ran, his mind had started shifting from Dee Kelley to Carly Bradford. More than anything, he wanted to help them both. And he wondered if his reluctance to believe that the shoes had belonged to Carly indicated a lack of hope for Carly or a lack of confidence in Dee's recovery.

Tyler's pace slowed, and he looked down at Patty, who panted hard. "Neither, right? I can't lose hope in either."

The dog tipped her head up once to look at him, then returned her focus to the street in front of her.

But the shoes can't be Carly's! We went over that ground with a fine-tooth comb. There's no way we missed something as important as her shoes! He stopped and bent over, bracing his hands on his knees and stretching his back and thighs. "Right?" he asked Patty again.

Patty decided a telephone pole was more interesting and tugged on her leash. He relented and as he waited ran his hand through his close-cropped hair, his deep-seated frustration rising again. His jogs normally pushed it away, but not today. He let out a long breath and resumed walking.

As he turned onto his street, a dark, nondescript sedan pulled up next to him, and the passenger window slid down. Fletcher leaned over and called to him. "Get in. We've been looking for you."

Tyler opened the back door and motioned for Patty to get in, then he got in the front. "What's going on?"

Fletcher turned the car toward downtown. "Wayne called the lodge when he couldn't get you on the phone. Someone's found Carly's dress."

FOUR

Thin bands of white moonlight brightened Dee's room and fell in stripes across her face. She stirred and blinked, easing awake in the silent room, confused as to why the moon seemed to be in the wrong position. The bed, the night table, also wrong. She jerked up as a short burst of panic flared in her. *Where am I?* The jerk produced pain in her face, neck and shoulders, and it all flooded back again—the day, the attack, the fuzzy ride home from the hospital.

Oh. Right. The lodge house, not my cabin. Dee pressed her head against the pillow and closed her eyes, aware that the pain, dull and throbbing, must have awakened her. She touched her face gingerly, a bit surprised at how much even the lightest touch hurt. Twin tears slipped from the corner of each eye, moistening her temples and disappearing into her hair.

What was I thinking, why didn't I just drop the sandals? Stupid! He could have killed me. Yet, even as she scolded herself, Dee knew why.

Carly. Whoever attacked her must have Carly. Dee now knew that fact as certainly as she knew her own name. No one else would know yet that she had found the shoes. No one else could know whether they were really Carly's. No matter how crazy it sounded, it had to be true. They *were* Carly's.

But would Tyler believe her? She'd seen the look in his eyes, and that doctor's, when she'd told the story in the E.R. They thought she was crazy.

Still crazy. Tyler must think I've had a relapse. Maybe I have. Dee did know she couldn't get Carly out of her head. She'd thought of almost nothing since she'd found the sandals. In and out of her grogginess at the hospital and, later, here, her mind had replayed every newspaper article she'd read, every television report she'd seen. *Carly is eight, the same age Joshua was. We have to find her. We have to!*

Dee knew that Carly now threatened to be lodged in her mind and spirit, almost in the same way Joshua had been. And Mickey. Even after they died. *But Carly... Carly might still be alive. And that—person—knows. I know what I heard. I heard it. I didn't make it up. He has to believe me.*

"Tyler," she whispered. Dee opened her eyes as she remembered the trip home, how he'd lifted her at the hospital, then again here. Lifted her as easily as if she were a child. He'd been so tender with her, as if she were fragile as well as injured. His chest and arms had been firm, radiating a comforting warmth, and he'd smelled like.... Dee closed her eyes again and inhaled, as if he were still next to her. He smelled like soap and freshly cut wood.

And there was something else...a whispered phrase. Even now she felt uncertain that she'd actually heard it.

Ride easy, Dixie Dee.

She smiled, which hurt, making her thoughts return to Carly. "You have to believe me." Her words slipped away unheard as sleep took over again, and she drifted away with one last thought. *I have to talk to the Bradfords.*

"Where?" Tyler demanded as Fletcher put the car in gear.

"Downstream from where Dee found the shoes. That stream apparently runs behind a subdivision a few miles down—"

"Ryan's Point. It's one of the older neighborhoods in Mercer. Some of the houses date back to the nineteenth century."

"A woman found it in her garbage bin. Said she'd noticed someone in her backyard earlier, but didn't think anything about it at first. Then she went to take out the trash, opened the bin, and there it was. She knew it wasn't hers and had seen enough of the news that she called the station. Wayne caught the call."

"Is he at the scene now?"

Fletcher took another turn and speeded up. "On his way." The older detective's mouth twisted into a wry smile. "Said the woman told him she'd seen enough of those true crime TV shows that she knew not to touch anything. Maybe they are good for something."

Tyler snorted. "Now if they'd stop convincing jurors that DNA is the answer to everything. Who's the woman?"

Fletcher pulled a slip of paper from his shirt pocket and handed it to Tyler, who unfolded it. Directions to the house, scribbled in Fletcher's bold, angular scrawl, cluttered most of the page. At the bottom, capital letters spelled out "Jenna Czock." Tyler said the name.

"You know her?"

"I know everybody in Mercer."

Fletcher's mouth twisted. "Small-town cop. I need to get you into New York sometime. I meant more than by sight."

"Nah, there are too many strangers in New York. Jenna runs the florist shop on Fourth, which she started after her divorce about twenty, twenty-five years ago, so my mother tells me. Jenna's maybe mid-fifties, dark hair. I don't know her well, but she sometimes eats lunch at Laurie's the same time Dee and I do."

Fletcher glanced sideways at his friend. "You and Dee eat lunch together?"

Tyler felt his cheeks burn. "I mean, we eat there at the same time. It's not like—" He broke off, stumbling over the explanation and deciding to change the subject. He didn't want to explain that he'd started timing his lunches so he'd be there when Dee arrived. "You need to turn here." He pointed.

"Directions said—"

"This is faster."

Fletcher followed Tyler's instructions, letting a few seconds of silence pass. "You know, I can be distracted, but I don't forget."

"Take the next left. We need to focus on the case."

In the silence that followed, Patty stuck her head between the front seats and Tyler scratched her chin. "OK. Go ahead and say it."

Fletcher remained silent.

Tyler filled in the empty air. "This makes Dee's claim a lot more credible." He pointed at another street.

Fletcher turned the corner, still quiet.

"Do you have any idea when I'll stop screwing up

this case? I should have jumped on those shoes and got them to the lab last night."

Fletcher glanced sideways again, then back to the road. "Don't give yourself so much credit. You're not screwing up anymore than the rest of us. This case is a jumbled mess and has been since Day One. You were right *not* to send the shoes last night. You know as well as I do how many false reports we've had about the shoes. It would be worse to jump the gun on these, especially given how fragile Nancy Bradford is right now. We need to find out if they *are* Carly's before we stir anything else up." Fletcher took a deep breath. "What I want to know is why pieces of Carly Bradford's last known set of clothes are suddenly being scattered up and down the same stream of water."

Tyler's gut twisted. "She's dead, and her killer is getting rid of evidence."

"But if Dee is right, then the shoes were a mistake. They weren't meant to be dropped. Her attacker was trying to get them back."

A sliver of hope rose again in Tyler. "But…once they were found and turned over to us, we'd know Carly might still be in the area. We'd renew our search for her. This time maybe even more intensively."

Fletcher turned the car into a subdivision and slowed, searching for the right street. "So the best way to keep us busy is to leave a trail leading in the wrong direction. A distraction."

Tyler stared at his friend. "She's going to be moved."

Fletcher nodded. "Most likely. And if we're not careful, it'll happen while we're peering into trash cans and following accident victims to the hospital."

Tyler let out a long sigh as Fletcher parked the car

behind Wayne's cruiser. "Then we need to move on the shoes quickly. I'll call Rick when we're through here."

"We're definitely going to need his resources as well as any manpower he can spare."

Tyler nodded and got out of the car. Rick Davis was the FBI special agent who had worked with them on the initial investigation. The FBI didn't usually investigate local cases of missing children unless there was absolute proof of foul play or immediate danger to the child. There had been no Amber alert on Carly for the same reason. Children who disappear into the woods don't usually have help doing so. They get lost; they have accidents. Tyler, however, put in a request for the FBI to help with the case as soon as he was convinced Carly hadn't just wandered off. His officers, the FBI and the local press turned the town into a fortress. The square-foot-by-square-foot search of the town lasted ten days. As the time passed, hope drained from the town and the officers. Rick and his team had finally left when they found themselves sitting around the police station one day doing nothing but reviewing old files and going through the interview transcripts yet one more time. There wasn't even enough evidence for a profile of a suspect. The case had simply come to an absolute dead end.

As if Carly had just vanished from the face of the earth. Until now.

Jenna Czock waited for them on the front stoop of her two-story Federal-style house. The boxlike home sat close to the road, but had a backyard comprising almost an acre of land. To the right of the house, a separate, more modern garage had a dark blue, mid-size sedan in front of it.

They pulled up behind it and got out, leaving the windows down for Patty. At Tyler's strict "Stay!" the dog stretched out on the backseat. Jenna came down the steps to greet them, looking like someone who'd just gotten home from work, with her red oxford cloth shirt, charcoal-gray slacks, and the thick makeup some older women seemed to prefer. A fleeting smile creased a worried face, and she motioned for them to follow her around the side of the house. She used a flashlight to augment the flood lights that shone from beneath the eaves of the house.

"I hated to bother you, and I'm hoping this isn't what I think…that it's just trash. I usually check the can just to see if there's room for another bag, and this was on top, just lying there. I've been following the case and listening to what the folks are saying around town. Everyone's still talking about that precious little girl."

They reached the back of the house, and Jenna pointed at a latticework cage set back from the house about forty feet. "The cans stay back there. I had that built for the garbage and the firewood. Cuts down on the raccoons in the garbage and the snow on the fire-wood."

Raccoons, indeed, thought Tyler. *This backyard must be a haven for them.* Towering old trees dotted the richly green and well-tended lawn, many of them surrounded by flowerbeds ripe with new spring flowers. The cage, with its slanted roof, had vines of clematis and morning glories running up its sides, allowing it to blend into the landscape. The yard had a gentle but steady slope from the house to the stream at the back of the property. Yellow dots of fireflies danced among the bushes at the edge of the water.

"People walk their dogs along the stream almost every day." Jenna pointed to a well-worn path that edged the water. "Even after dark like this. And there are two hiking trails on the other side that run close." She shrugged and hugged herself as she followed them toward the cage, where Wayne had set up a bright spot-light on a tall mount. "It's just not unusual to see people in my backyard, but I should have realized this one was up closer than most. I just didn't dream someone would get into my garbage."

"Man or woman?"

Jenna shrugged. "Not sure. It was already pretty dark. It looked as if they were wearing a cap, maybe sweats. Somewhere between my height and yours, I guess."

"So about five-nine, five-ten."

Jenna nodded. "I'm five-eight, so yes."

They rounded the edge of the lattice, to find Wayne bent over next to the cage's opening, peering at the ground illuminated by the white light of the quartz spot he had set up. He spoke without greeting. "Only one set of prints, but it's been pretty dry the last couple of days. Doesn't match either of the sets in the woods."

Tyler cleared his throat, and Wayne looked up at Tyler, puzzled, then his gaze darted to Jenna and back to his boss.

Jenna perked up. "In the woods?" She grabbed Tyler's elbow. "Does this have anything to do with Dee being attacked this morning?"

Fletcher let out a long sigh and squatted next to Wayne. "Small town."

Before Tyler could respond, Jenna bolted on. "Phil, down at the convenience store, had the scanner on this morning, heard it and called his sister, she works at the hospital, saw Dee in the E.R. Is she OK?"

Tyler patted her hand. "She'll be fine. Just a few scratches."

"Is she back at the retreat?"

Tyler nodded. "But—"

"I should send her some flowers. Roses, do you think?"

"Maybe—"

"Or tulips. I think she said one time in the café that she likes tulips. You know, she talked about how she used to grow tulips and—"

Fletcher straightened and cut off Jenna's rapid words. "Ms. Czock, would you mind if I got a glass of water?"

Jenna paused in her flower review and smiled. "Certainly. Follow me, and I'll show you where the glasses are." She took his arm, and they turned for the house.

Once they were out of earshot, Wayne also rose. "Sorry," he muttered.

Tyler waved away the apology. "I shouldn't have let her follow us down here. The whole town will know about the connection today." He reached to adjust his hat, then realized he didn't have it on. "What do you have?"

Wayne pointed a gloved hand at the open Dumpster-type receptacle. "The dress is spread out as if it's on display."

Tyler looked. The blue gingham dress lay draped across two plastic garbage bags, one of which had been ripped open, so that paper, eggshells and days-old milk had leaked out into the can and over the dress. Tyler winced at the odor. "So the kidnapper intended for it to be found."

"I think so. If he had wanted to hide it or just dispose of it, it would have been simpler just to shove it down in the can beneath the bags."

"A message. But why here? Why not leave it on a bench in town or some other place like that?"

"My guess is that it would be too risky. Someone might see it, or the dress could be picked up. Here it's protected, yet it's doused in a forensic soup. No way we're going to get an uncontaminated clue out of this. Since Jenna's the florist, her hours and routine are easy to determine. And he knew that Jenna would be following the case and would spot it right away."

Both men stood silent for a moment, then Wayne cleared his throat. "I've finished processing everything I could. I'm ready to bag it."

Tyler nodded and stepped back, watching as Wayne eased the dress out of the garbage with a pair of tongs and slipped it into a brown paper bag. "Any blood?"

Wayne shook his head. "Not that I could see. You know it'll take weeks to process this at the lab."

"I'd rather they be thorough than quick. We've made enough mistakes already in this case."

Wayne paused and looked his boss over carefully. "Not anymore than another team might have. Why are you being so hard on yourself with this?"

Tyler's eyes narrowed. "Because Jack and Nancy Bradford are still missing their eight-year-old daughter."

Wayne opened his mouth to respond, but a door slammed, and they turned to see Fletcher and Jenna returning. Jenna smiled at them as they entered the light cast by the spot, but the stoic Fletcher showed no emotion at all. Tyler focused on Jenna, slipping his fingers around her arm and pulling her to his side. He lowered his voice as he pointed to the trash can. "Jenna, we're done here, but you know we'd appreciate it if you would keep this to yourself for a bit. We don't want any wild speculations getting back to Jack and Nancy before we have a chance to talk with them. You know how it is."

Jenna glowed at his confidence in her, as he had hoped. "Of course, Tyler. I'll keep it quiet until you say otherwise." She held up two fingers. "Scout's honor."

"Thank you." Tyler released her and motioned Wayne and Fletcher to follow him. They remained silent as they returned to the cars. Wayne left with the evidence he'd gathered as Tyler and Fletcher settled into the sedan. Tyler scratched the patient Patty behind her ears, barely glancing at his friend as they fastened their seat belts and left the house.

Tyler finally cleared his throat. "Everything okay?"

Fletcher gave a quick nod. "That woman talks more than anyone I've met in a long time. And clingy. She never left my side. Kept trying to pump me for info." He rolled his shoulders, as if to push away the encounter.

Tyler fought a smile. This wasn't the first time Fletcher's striking Eurasian looks had gotten him unwanted attention. Women around Mercer found Fletcher to be both handsome and exotic, and some never resisted the temptation to flirt shamelessly. Such attention, however, never failed to annoy the happily married detective. "I appreciate you getting her away from the scene. See anything *else* suspicious in the house?"

Fletcher glanced at him, then finally grinned. He

straightened his shoulders, as if to shake off the last of Jenna's advances. "No. The kitchen and living room were clean, just the usual clutter of a house that's actually used. Not a lot of light. She said she'd been cleaning, and the dishwasher was running. She went on about how expensive the heating oil had been this winter, and that she was having trouble with air in her pipes making them rattle. She talked about her daughter, told me she'd been following Carly's story."

Tyler looked out the window at the passing suburban houses. They all looked so...*normal...*"Yeah. Elaine. Wayne and I discussed that might be why the kidnapper left the dress with her."

"She said any mother worth her salt would be watching around every corner."

"Like Dee."

"You think it was her mother's instinct that made Dee fight for the sandals?"

Tyler nodded. "She's still a bit of a wounded bird, as you well know. Stronger, but the idea of losing a child resonates deeply with her."

Fletcher swung the car through a turn and headed for downtown Mercer. "You want me to drop you at the house or the station?"

"The station. I'll make sure Wayne doesn't need anything else from me right now, then walk home. Patty's been patient, so I'm sure she'd love a chance to stretch her legs."

Fletcher pulled into a parking spot in front of the storefront office, and Tyler got out, snapping his fingers for Patty, who bounded out of the car and halfway up the block and back before Tyler could reach the door. The Mercer police station, a converted storefront, had been both a dime store and a bank in years gone by. Now it held Mercer's tiny force of five officers, a dispatcher, and Wayne, who did double duty as detective and crime scene specialist. One of their three dispatchers always sat behind the front desk to greet visitors and direct them to the proper officer for a complaint. A cheaply paneled wall separated the front from the bull pen area where the officers and Wayne had desks. The wall extended the width of the building, creating a front hall and waiting area.

Two doors in the wall allowed access to the back. One led to the bull pen. The other opened onto a narrow hallway leading to the police chief's office and two interrogation rooms.

A bell clanged over Tyler's head as he pulled the door open, and the third-shift dispatcher, Sally, looked up. She acknowledged her boss with a nod of the head toward the bull pen door. "Wayne beat you back by about five minutes. Anything I can do?"

"Thanks. Think we're covered." He entered the bull pen, Patty trotting behind him. Normally silent at this hour, the room echoed with Wayne's shuffling evidence bags and paperwork. Tyler sat down next to his desk. "You going to stay long?"

Wayne shook his head. "I'm going to lock everything in my desk, then e-mail the lab to let them know I'm sending the dress and shoes tomorrow."

"Take them."

Wayne paused in his work. "What?"

"I want you to deliver them. I'll call Rick before I leave and see if his folks can put a little pressure on the process."

"You sure?"

"Yes. Tomorrow will mostly be spent with the Bradfords. I want to show them the shoes and dress first thing. Then you can take them."

Wayne hesitated. "Show them before—"

"They'll know whether they're Carly's."

"Tyler, I don't—"

"Tyler." The sharp voice interrupted them, cutting through the deliberation. They turned toward the door, where Sally stood, distress on her face. She continued without pausing. "The security alarm at the retreat is going off."

FIVE

The alarm siren sliced through Dee's brain, blurring her vision and making her teeth ache. Dizzy from the pain of the attack as well as the alarm, she pressed her hands over her ears as she braced herself in the doorway leading from the hall into the lodge's great room. Moonlight laced through the windows, creating stark bands of silver light throughout the room, while the lights that ringed the house flashed like yellow, disco-era strobe lights.

Near the door, Maggie frantically entered the alarm code into a keypad with one hand, while the other clutched a baseball bat. Both hands trembled furiously, but she succeeded. The alarm went silent and the outside lights stopped flashing. She turned on the inside lights, and the women looked at each other. Maggie swallowed hard and renewed a two-handed grip on the bat. "Are you okay?"

Dee nodded once, then whispered, "Where's Fletcher?"

"Still with Tyle—"

Maggie's words broke off as the front door burst open. They both screamed, whirling toward it. Fletcher stood there, gun drawn. His gaze swept the room, then focused on his wife. "You all right?" His voice, low and guttural, sounded like a drum in Dee's ears, and her knees felt weak. Stumbling forward, she fumbled for one of the soft chairs near the fireplace on the front wall and sank down into it.

Instead of answering Fletcher, Maggie nodded toward the back door, which stood open. Following her lead, Fletcher exited cautiously onto the back deck, scanning all around him. Maggie watched him go, then a horrified look crossed her face as a raw wail echoed through the house. "David!" She fled down the hall on the other side of the great room, toward her baby son.

Dee drew her knees up to her chest and pushed deeper into the chair, confusion clouding her mind and adrenaline making her shiver. She realized that her thoughts remained locked in a swirl because of the painkillers she'd taken, but she couldn't blame the drugs for the maelstrom of emotions within her. A black fear blended with a stark sense of loss yanked her back to the dark days following Mickey and Joshua's deaths, when daily she felt as if she were being pulled into a bottomless pit.

"I can't do this again." Her choked voice sounded flat and unfamiliar, as if it were not her own, and the fear spiked again. This time Dee realized the fear came not from the alarm or the attack but from deep within. A fear that this would push her back to the chasm of grief that she had dwelled in for so long.

No. *No!* "I've come too far." She hugged her knees tighter but cleared her throat. "I've come too far."

"Dee?"

Startled, she jerked toward the front door, and an odd sense of total relief flooded her at the sight of Tyler filling the doorway. In his shorts and T-shirt, he looked strikingly normal—and strong. Dee had never realized that his uniform camouflaged how strong he really was. She released her knees and pointed at the back door. "Fletcher went out on the deck."

He nodded, but instead crossed to her rapidly. "My men are circling around." He dropped to one knee and took her hands in his. "How are you doing?"

Tyler's grip was warm and comforting, and more of the tension eased out of her body. She nodded. "I'm okay." At his look of doubt, she looked down at their hands and realized he could feel her trembling. "Shaky, but okay. The adrenaline."

"Any idea what set off the alarm?"

She shook her head, but Maggie's "Not yet" caused them both to turn. Emerging from the hall, Maggie pressed David's body against hers, and he murmured softly into her shoulder as his thumb found his mouth. "We haven't had time to search the house, but it's not that big. I bet anyone trying to get in ran off when the alarm sounded."

"No doubt."

"Maggie." Fletcher came back in, his gun still in one hand. He pointed toward the backyard. "We can't see anyone out back, and the writers are starting to gather. Can you talk to them, get them to go back to their cabins? Tyler's men are still out there."

Tyler stood. "We need to search the house."

Fletcher nodded at him. "True. You start with that wing." He hesitated, then lovingly touched David's back as he spoke again to Maggie. "You're probably safer with the deputies. Stay with one of them until I give the all clear."

And with that, Dee was alone again, as Tyler disappeared down the hallway where her bedroom was, and Fletcher searched the rooms on the opposite side of the great room. She curled up in the chair again and pulled a lush throw from across the back down onto her legs. Despite the warmth of the weather, she felt chilled.

Maggie was right; searching the house shouldn't take long. While larger than any home Dee had ever lived in, the retreat's lodge had been designed for comfort and practicality, not luxury. The large great room was both living and dining room, with a sitting area near a fireplace at the front and a dining table that sat sixteen at the back. A kitchen with an open counter was located on the south side, and two hallways on opposite sides led to four rooms each. In addition to the kitchen, on the south hallway were Maggie's office, her and Fletcher's bedroom, and David's nursery. Three rooms on the north hall were all bedrooms, two for guests and one for the groundskeeper—a woman named Julie, who kept to herself so completely that the writers only saw her at dinner. The fourth room was a laundry open to all the residents.

The steps leading downstairs also led off the north hallway. The game room downstairs held a bar, pool table, and video games, as well as the only television set at the retreat. A narrow loft over the great room held a public computer with Internet access and research materials.

Both men returned quickly, and Tyler glanced once at Dee, then spoke to Fletcher in low tones. The older man turned and went out the front door as Tyler returned, sitting in the chair closest to Dee.

"Dee, did you hear anything before the alarm went off?"

She searched his face, suspicious. "Why?"

Tyler stared down at his hands for a moment, clenching them into fists once, then relaxing. He inhaled deeply, then looked at her again. "The window in your room has been tampered with, as if someone tried to pry it open from the outside. Apparently, when that didn't succeed, they risked the back door. That's what set off the alarm."

An icy wave of fear flooded over Dee, and she clutched the throw tighter. "Why? Why me?"

Tyler closed his hands over hers and leaned closer, his voice tender and low. "I don't know. There's a possibility this is random, just coincidence. You had the bedroom on the front. It's the window closest to the ground."

Watching Tyler's face, feeling the heat of his hands on hers, a tenuous sense of peace settled over her. "You don't believe that it's unrelated, do you?"

He hesitated, then shook his head. "No. I'm not a fan of coincidences of any kind, and there's never been a break-in here."

Her mouth twisted. "A burglar would have to be an idiot to try here. Fletcher's armed, and the writers prowl the grounds at all hours of the night when their writing isn't going well. But I still don't get why he would come after me."

"Maybe he thought you still had the shoes."

"But—"

Tyler's grip tightened around her fingers. "Don't try to make sense of it right now. It's still too early to reason it through. Not enough evidence."

Fletcher stepped back through the front door and motioned for Tyler.

"I'll be right back," he whispered as he stood. The

two men conferred in soft voices that made it impossible for her to understand the words.

Instead, Dee watched Tyler, trying to figure out why the fear that had swarmed over her, the darkness that remained a threat just at the edge of her awareness, slipped away whenever he came near. That didn't make sense either. Nothing did, and her thoughts swirled in a fog again, frustrating her. *These painkillers!* She looked down and fingered her bandages lightly, testing the pain, and found her wounds still tender to the touch. She knew she should continue the pills, at least through tomorrow, but she hated being like this, dazed and foggy. From the moment she'd realized the shoes were Carly's, she'd felt the drive to *do* something. Help. That feeling hadn't gone away, not even after the attack, the drugs.

I want to talk to the Bradfords.

Dee took a deep breath and pushed the throw aside and stood up.

Tyler appeared at her side instantly, taking her arm. "What are you doing?"

"I want to talk to the Bradfords."

Tyler stood quite still for a moment, his eyes widening for a moment, then narrowing. Clearly, that was not what he'd expected her to say. He studied her, then licked his lips. "Dee, it's close to midnight. I hope they're asleep."

She shook her head once, ignoring a sudden pain in her left cheek. "They won't be. This is when it wakes you up. Always."

It. The grief. The fear. The scant remaining hope. The nightmares. The chasm of loss.

He didn't ask. In fact, he nodded slightly and stood

straighter, as if he understood. But he didn't relent. "But they need each other, not to be interrupted when it's the rawest."

Dee stared, her breath caught in her throat. He *did* get it. She exhaled slowly. "Then tomorrow."

He nodded. "We'll talk about it tomorrow. Right now, we have some crime scene details to take care of. We could move you and Maggie to a hotel, but I think you'll be safer here. Obviously, reaction to intruders here is pretty swift and thorough. We're moving you across the hall so you can rest while we finish."

"And the window is higher off the ground."

He lifted one shoulder in a shrug. "It has its advantages."

Dee put one hand on his arm. "Tyler, whatever it is I'm afraid of, it's not a person. Not really."

He nodded, then reached up and gently touched her cheek. "I know. If it were, you would have dropped the shoes."

Safe.

She'd been attacked, drugged, and had her temporary "home" violated. Yet for the first time in three years, Dee Kelley felt the fear truly slip away, not just a feeling that was held at bay for a moment, still looking over her shoulder. In this man's presence, looking into his eyes, it dissipated, like fog in the glare of the morning sun.

With Tyler, she was safe.

SIX

Carly watched the moonlight creep slowly across her window, unable to go back to sleep. Her captor had returned almost an hour ago, the rage in full flower, and the screams, thuds and crashes echoed through the overhead vent and shook the ceiling. Carly had waited, fear freezing her to the bed, for the sound of boots on the stairs, but they never came. Even though the silence had lasted a long time, Carly couldn't sleep.

Cool white light filled the room, and she looked around, once again, at her strange prison. The window, barely eight inches high and a foot wide, let in the only light from outside. The room, though spotless and neatly decorated, smelled damp and a bit moldy. The walls were painted a delicate lavender, and the white bed and dresser were the perfect size for a young girl. A toy box sat in one corner, loaded down with dolls and other playthings, but Carly had not touched them, much to the dismay of her captor.

A child's desk in the corner under the ceiling vent still held art supplies, but Carly hadn't touched them in several days. She'd drawn a few pictures in the beginning, but her captor took them away, acting proud of them, which made Carly feel even worse. She wasn't about to do anything that made her captor happy.

Her dinner tray still sat on the dresser, forgotten in her captor's rush to get out of the house tonight. An old black-and-white television sat next to the tray, but it barely picked up two local channels. Boring.

Less boring were the books that filled a small case near the dresser. They were as old as the toys, but Carly knew some of the titles, and her mother had read several to her when she was younger. These helped. *The Secret Garden. Anne of Green Gables. Big Red. Queenie Peavy.* Several Nancy Drew books. These reminded her that kids in trouble usually got out of it.

Carly swallowed. She had to get out of it, too. She stood up on the bed and stepped up on the headboard, careful with her balance. She'd figured out that if she braced one hand on the wall and grabbed the window frame with the other, she could tiptoe high enough to see out the window. She wasn't strong enough to stay in that position long, but at least she could see out sometimes.

The window looked out on a large yard, and tonight the bright moon turned the bushes and trees into hulking towers casting black shadows over the lawn. The glittering eyes of a cat shone from beneath one of the bushes as it hunted.

Carly's muscles trembled from the strain, and she dropped back down on the bed. Her mind wandered to the books again. *I'm a princess who's been captured, but who will rescue me? Or how do I rescue myself?*

She got up, snapped on the lamp near the bed, and went to the bookcase.

* * *

Tyler punched his pillow again, but his restlessness bit deep. The red numbers on his bedside clock constantly reminded him of how close dawn was and how far away any semblance of sleep. He had finally left the lodge house around three, just as Wayne had finished his work outside. Photographs and fingerprints had been taken, as well as one cast of a footprint, which Fletcher and Wayne both said looked a lot like one they had found near the site of Dee's attack.

His frustration at his inability to see the clear path of this crime—starting with the motive for it—had intensified today to the point of anger. He'd even woken Rick Davis out of a deep sleep to ask for his help tonight, only to find out that Rick and his team had moved on to another case. No help for now. They were on their own for a few days, possibly weeks. The hard truth was that there were too many missing kids and not enough law enforcement. Even the FBI was stretched thin. Civilian groups, many of whom ran predator or missing child Web sites, helped, but not this time. Every tip, every hint, led only to a dead end.

He rolled over on his back and stared at the ceiling. Patty glared at him, then hopped off the foot of the bed and stretched out under the window.

"Lord," he muttered, "this is impossible."

Unbidden, a memory flashed through his mind, the look on Dee's face when she announced, "I want to talk to the Bradfords." His heart had ached when he first saw her, covered in bandages and folded in on herself in that chair, like a wounded animal trying to hide from a predator. Yet every time he touched her tonight, Dee had seemed to "unfold" emotionally a bit, more and more, until she had made that pronouncement.

So maybe this wasn't going to be the psychological setback for her that he had feared.

"Lord, help us both."

And while Tyler believed with all his heart that prayer would be answered, right now he couldn't see how that answer would come. "Just have to trust," he said, swinging his legs off the bed. Couldn't sleep; might as well work. He dressed, fed a confused Patty, then headed out to his car. The clock on the wall behind Sally's head had just clicked past five when he let himself in the front door.

She stifled a yawn. "Couldn't sleep?"

He shook his head. "Too wound up. You go on home. Mom will be in soon. I'll catch the phones if they ring before that." Tyler's mother, Peg, handled the dispatch and receptionist work during the first shift, just as she had for the past twenty years.

Sally stood up, glad for the relief. "Thanks. They've been quiet since you and Wayne left."

"Thanks. Get some rest."

Tyler went into the bull pen to make coffee, then took a hot cup into his office. He closed the door and sat down, staring at the phone. It was too early to call anyone. Besides, calling the Bradfords with anything but good news made his gut ache and burn. Since the main search had been called off, Nancy and Jack had disappeared behind the walls of their big house and hadn't talked to anyone, even close friends. It irked every last nerve that he could no longer justify the expense of an extensive search, and he'd contemplated suggesting to them that they hire Fletcher as a private detective.

Tyler knew Fletcher could find a black cat at

midnight, if he set his mind to it. The man's fifteen years with the NYPD had given him a wealth of experience and a network of crime scene experts that would do anything for him. Fletcher had been visiting his best friend, Aaron Jackson, two years ago, when Aaron was murdered. Fletcher investigated—and solved—the crime. In the process, he'd fallen hard for Maggie and had eventually moved to Mercer and married her. To Tyler's great relief, Fletcher often worked with him and the Mercer PD as a consultant.

Fletcher, however, had preferred working with the PD privately on this one. His reasoning was simple: "You're doing everything possible with the case. The FBI couldn't find anything. I can't add to that now. Carly is either already dead, or she'll be alive for a while longer. We'll keep working at the top of our game."

"He thinks this is local," Tyler muttered, picking up the picture of Carly from his desk. "Please let her be alive."

Reluctantly, Tyler set the picture aside and turned to his computer. He started his usual morning routine, although today he began a few hours earlier than normal. The Mercer PD had set up a Web site for tips, as had the Bradfords, both emphasizing the $100,000 reward her parents had put up for finding her and smaller rewards for information. The local media had kept Carly's story on the front pages of their sites, encouraging tips in their comment sections. He went through his e-mail for updates from volunteer armchair detectives in all the surrounding states and Canada. Finally, he searched for her name on the Internet, wading through pages of junk for any clue.

Nothing. One more day of nothing. Nothing!

He tipped his cup, which had long since been empty and cold, to double check for any last drops of caffeine. With a sigh, he stood and went for more. It was almost 8:30, and a second pot had already been brewed, filling the room with the stimulating aroma. Peg had settled in up front, and two of his officers greeted him as they prepped for their shift, making small talk about their nights and their anticipations for the weekend. One of them inquired about the alarm, and Tyler filled them in, asking them, as he did every morning, to be alert for signs of Carly.

Returning to his office with his coffee, he sank into his chair. *When, Lord, did looking for a missing child become part of our morning routine?* He rubbed his eyes, knowing his call couldn't wait. He reached for the receiver. *Help me, Father,* he thought, as he punched in a telephone number he knew by heart. He waited as the phone rang, two…three…four times. Under his desk, his right leg began to bounce, a gesture that was part tension relief, part anxiety. When the Bradfords' answering machine picked up, he hesitated. This was not information to leave on a machine. He took a deep breath as the beep sounded.

"Jack, Nancy, this is Tyler Madison. Would you please—"

"Tyler! Jack here. Hang on, hang on, let me cut this thing off." Sounds of scrambling echoed hollowly in Tyler's ear, then the sounds of the open line softened. "Tyler, do you have news? Anything?"

Tyler pressed a fist down on his leg to stop the bouncing. "Maybe. Could I come out to see you later this morning? I need to ask you some questions."

"Of course!" Jack paused and cleared his throat. His voice dropped in tone. "Yes. Nancy's still asleep, but she'll be up shortly. She's…she's not sleeping at night, so the doctor has put her on a sedative. It's not good, Tyler. I think it'll help to see you. Talk to you about Carly again."

Tyler squeezed his eyes shut. *Please don't get your hopes up again.* "I hope so. I'm going to bring Fletcher with me. That okay?" Jack and Fletcher had gotten to know each other fairly well during the initial stages of the search. With a new baby in the house, Fletcher now shared every parent's fear of a missing child, a fear that had turned to truth with the Bradfords. Fletcher had been on the scene every day.

"Sure."

"Give us about an hour. See you then." Tyler eased the receiver back into its cradle and released a breath he had not realized he'd been holding. He placed his palms flat on the desk and forced himself to stand, whispering as he did so. "Okay, God, keep Your hands on us. I really don't want to hurt the Bradfords anymore than they already have been. Ready to keep me from falling on my face?"

A soft knock on his door got his attention, then Peg stuck her head in. "Fletcher's here. Dee's with him. He took her into interrogation room one, if you want to join in."

Tyler moved from behind the desk. "Good idea." He took a right turn out of his office and walked the five feet or so to the next room. While they still needed to get her statement about yesterday, he'd hoped she would rest this morning, and he had said so last night to Fletcher. Plus, he didn't look forward to explaining to Dee that she couldn't go with them to the Bradfords. Obviously, Fletcher had had no success keeping her at the retreat, which surprised Tyler. He'd seen Fletcher interrogate people before, and he knew how persuasive the detective could be.

When he walked in the door, however, he almost laughed, thinking Fletcher might need all the help he could get. Fletcher MacAllister, the product of a Thai mother and Scottish father, stood more than a foot taller than the petite woman in front of him and outweighed her by probably 80 pounds. Yet he was the one with his back against the wall, his arms crossed defensively. His dark, silky hair flopped over his forehead as he stared down at Dee, his eyebrows raised in surprise.

Dee had her hands on her hips, head tipped back so she could stare at Fletcher eye-to-eye. As she spoke, she rocked up on her toes with every other word or so, giving the impression she was about to fall against Fletcher's chest. Clearly her painkillers from last night had worn off, although she still wore the bandages on her face.

They reminded Tyler of a picture he'd seen of a determined Chihuahua confronting a resolute Great Dane. A Chihuahua with one black eye.

Her eyes sparked with anger. "Don't you get sanctimonious with me, Fletcher MacAllister. You can't imagine what Carly's parents feel unless you've been there, unless you've had your child ripped out of your arms forever. Don't lay the faults in this investigation on a lack of money or time or team. Preposterous. I've run enough fund-raisers in my life to know that when the cause is right, people will turn their pockets inside out, if need be. And I *should* go with you. I know what they're going through! Has anyone from the county talked to them about counseling? Has anyone other than cops or the press sat down with them to really talk about how they feel, how they're doing with this kind of loss? Has anyone—?"

"Dee."

She acknowledged Tyler's presence only with a slight tip of her head to the left, but her words were still aimed at Fletcher. "Why isn't more being done to find that precious little girl!"

"Sit." The soft word still held enough of a command that Dee turned, and Tyler faced her solemnly. "You don't want Fletcher to be sanctimonious, yet you're very quick to assume that what you see publicly is all we're doing to find Carly." He pulled out a chair and motioned for her to sit.

"As you can see, you're in a private room for the very reason that I don't want anyone else knowing the details of what happened yesterday or anything that needs to be discussed this morning. Too many people already have a lot of misinformation.

"And after what you went through with your own accident investigation, you, of all people, should realize how much of an investigation takes place out of the public eye, even on a case like this."

Dee blinked, almost as if awakening from a dream, and sat slowly. "I do understand. But I don't see how—"

Tyler sat across from her and Fletcher moved to her left so he could see her face. "Tell us everything you remember about yesterday."

Dee straightened her shoulders and rested her hands on the table. "I found the shoes about a mile out, down the path. I was jogging from the retreat into town. My left calf started to cramp so I stopped to stretch it."

"Near the stream."

She nodded. "It was where the stream crosses under the path, near that wooden foot bridge. There's a grassy embankment coming up from the stream. Very shady. A good place to rest. I've stopped there before on my walks."

Tyler leaned over the table, focusing on her face. "How far were you from the logging road?"

"Maybe twenty yards on the other side of it. Toward the retreat."

Tyler's lips pursed, but he remained silent, as the hope he had that the shoes were Carly's wavered. The stream, the trail, and the logging road all were within a mile of the Bradfords' property. The stream ran through the woods behind their house. Because of that, the search for Carly had focused with a laser's intensity on those three areas. Dogs, officers and volunteers had combed every inch of the area several times, including that embankment.

The shoes had not been there in the days after Carly's disappearance. Even if they had missed them, it had rained a solid week last month, causing the stream to rise and leave the ground around it a muddy mess. The grass had only grown up again in the last two or three weeks, as the temperature had warmed and the rains ceased and the white sandals were still pristine. So if these *were* Carly's shoes, how did they get there? If Dee's attacker was the kidnapper, then there remained a strong possibility that Carly was alive and in the area. If so, how had they missed her? Tyler didn't know whether to hope...or feel more incompetent than ever.

Dee looked from one man to the other, her look of determination fading to concern. She licked her lips, then took a long breath. She sat straighter, and Tyler admired the way she seemed to be holding herself together. She met his gaze firmly. "I know you still doubt the sandals are Carly's, but they have to be. They *have* to be. Why else would that…person…attack me trying to get them back and the break-in? I know you think that was about the shoes."

Tyler hesitated, knowing he needed to tell her the rest. The attack added weight to her claim, but so did the dress. Yet nothing was certain until the Bradfords identified both. He glanced at Fletcher, who shrugged, then nodded once.

Dee caught both movements, and her gaze sharpened. "What's going on?"

Tyler took a deep breath and explained about finding Carly's dress. As he did, Dee's expression flared from curiosity to excitement. She grabbed Tyler's hands and almost came up out of her chair. "Then she's still alive! Carly's still alive!"

Fletcher pressed her back into her chair. "We don't know that, Dee. She could be, or the kidnapper could have dumped the dress to get rid of evidence as a sign that he's about to move her, or…" His voice trailed off.

"Or kill her," Tyler finished.

Dee grew still, studying him. After a moment, she tilted her head to one side, and her eyes narrowed. "Okay, then. What do we need to do to help the Brad-fords?"

Tyler fought a smile. *Where was all this determination coming from?* "First, I want you to finish telling us about yesterday. Then Nancy and Jack Bradford are going to have to identify the sandals and dress. That's essential, no matter what we think. If they're up to it, I'll take them out to their house. Then, we can—"

"Can I go with you?"

Tyler frowned. "No, I don't think—"

"But I know what they're going through better than anyone else. I can help."

"This will be an official visit—"

"But they might want to know where the sandals were found as well. They might know something about—"

"Dee. No." Tyler straightened, becoming more of the cop again. "You can't go this time." He almost grimaced, recognizing instantly that "this time" might have been a mistake.

It was. "Okay, not this time, but soon. I want to talk to them. I *need* to talk to them."

"Maybe, but—"

His mother opened the door, and Tyler had a sudden urge to hug her neck. "Sorry to interrupt, Tyler. The Bradfords are here. They said they couldn't wait."

Fletcher muttered something under his breath and turned away.

Tyler nodded at Peg. "Please put the Bradfords in room two. I'll get the shoes and dress from Wayne's evidence locker."

She nodded and left, and Tyler looked back at Dee. "I want you to go back to the retreat. I'll have one of the guys take you—"

"No."

His eyebrows went up. "What?"

She stood up and squared her shoulders. "You can let me be a part of this, or I'll talk to them without you.

I have to talk to them, Tyler. I *have* to. My way we all hear what's going on. Your way means someone's always out of the loop, and that's no way to find a child. What will it be?"

SEVEN

Tyler rubbed the back of his neck, and Dee noticed for the first time how dark the circles under his eyes were. *Wonder how much sleep he's had in the past three months.* She hated giving him the ultimatum, and she held her breath, terrified it would backfire on her. The cops she knew back home would have laughed or read her the riot act at such a demand. But she had to try. She had to be a part of this. They couldn't understand what the Bradfords were going through, not really. She did.

Tyler looked at Fletcher again, but Dee was afraid to turn her gaze away from him. "Please," she said softly.

He looked her over carefully, then finally said, "Sit in the corner. Don't speak. Don't emote. Don't move. Don't ask them anything until we're finished. Understand?"

She nodded, relief flooding through her.

He wasn't quite convinced. "Promise me."

Dee put a hand over her heart. "Not a word."

"Not a whimper."

"I promise."

He led them out of the room, and they waited in the

hall while he retrieved the two brown paper bags of evidence, which he handed to Fletcher. They entered the interrogation room where the Bradfords waited, and Tyler introduced Dee.

Jack Bradford had to be one of the most handsome men Dee had ever seen, with a firm jawline and blue-gray eyes. His rich, dark brown hair, neatly cut and soft, had natural streaks of auburn running through it that Dee knew would glisten red in the sun. His skin, smooth and evenly tanned, made his light eyes even more distinctive.

Nancy's eyes, however, were dark and brooding, pools of sadness in a face blotchy from crying and lack of sleep. Normally a woman whose olive-skinned Mediterranean beauty matched her husband's, Nancy was a walking portrayal of grief, with bloodshot eyes sunk into deep hollows and her muscles stretched with tension.

Jack stood immediately, his gaze going over Dee's face with a doctor's practiced eye. "You were the one who was attacked in the woods?"

Tyler and Fletcher exchanged an unreadable glance, but Dee focused on Jack. "Yes. How did you know?"

"I may not be at the hospital much these days, but I stay in touch with my staff about business. My office manager has a daughter doing a rotation in the E.R. She asked if I knew you."

"You," Nancy started, then faltered. She swallowed, then raised her hand toward Dee, who took it and held it close. "You're the one who lost your little boy."

Dee bit her upper lip to fight back the tears, then nodded. "Yes. Three years ago."

Confusion and apprehension clouded Jack's face. "What do you have to do with our Carly?"

Tyler's hands on Dee's shoulders were gentle but firm, and he guided her away from the table. She settled in a chair against the wall, trying only to keep watch. "We think Dee was attacked because of something she found in the woods, which may be evidence in this case."

Jack Bradford sat stiffly on the edge of his chair, and put a strong but slender hand flat on the table, his long fingers splayed wide, as if bracing himself for bad news. "What did she find?"

Tyler paused, then squared his shoulders. "We have, in fact, found a couple of items we need you to identify, if you can. Dee found a pair of white sandals—"

Both Bradfords sucked in air, and Tyler held up his hand, as Jack dropped back against his chair. "Please. I want to warn you before we do this. The place where the sandals were found had already been searched extensively. We also know that a lot of that style shoe had been sold this spring. They could easily belong to another child."

Jack nodded, his voice stern. "Show them."

Silently, Tyler took one of the bags from Fletcher and sat in the chair opposite the Bradfords. He slipped the sandals out and placed them on the table.

Nancy's elegantly manicured hand shook violently as she reached for the small shoes. A tall, distinguished woman who normally held herself erect with pride, Nancy had been crushed by her daughter's disappearance, and she now sat slumped in her chair, as if she were about to fall out of it. Jack put one arm around his wife, holding her tightly, as he let her look more closely at the shoes.

Dee watched the two of them, remembering she'd

heard that Jack had tried to return to his medical practice, but his time away from home remained limited. His main mission in life these days were his attempts to keep Nancy sane.

Nancy ran her quivering fingertips lightly over the shoes. "They do look so much…" Her voice trailed off as she turned them over and examined the soles more closely.

She gasped and the shoes slid from her hands, dropping to the table with a soft thump. Nancy turned and buried herself against her husband, sobbing. Wrapping one arm even tighter around her, Jack picked up the shoes and turned them over. His face revealed the same sense of recognition and he pushed them back toward Tyler. "The star on the bottom. That's not part of the shoes' design. Carly kept losing her shoes, especially in the summer, and so many do look alike." He paused, wrapping his free arm around Nancy as well. "Nancy started drawing those stars on the soles so we could tell which ones were Carly's." His voice cracked. "Nancy told her it was because she was our shining star." He leaned his head against his wife's, clearly fighting the tears as well.

They weren't alone. Dee swallowed hard, fighting to keep her promise to Tyler. Cascades of grief, anger and empathy washed over her. Snapshots of a laughing Joshua flashed in her head, followed by the sight of him lying gray and still on the pavement near their destroyed car. Tears slipped from her eyes, and she pressed a finger to her lips when Tyler reached for the dress.

He hesitated, holding the bag in front of him. His voice dropped into a tone that sounded both comforting but cautious. "This may be even harder, but I need you to look at it closely. Make sure it really belonged to Carly. It was found in a garbage bin, so the stains on it are normal soiling from the bin. Nothing appears to be linked to Carly's disappearance."

Dee held her breath. *He's trying to tell them the stains aren't blood,* she thought, surprised at his awareness of how a parent would think, the assumptions you could jump to when hoping for the best and expecting the worst.

Tyler slowly pulled the dress from the bag, and Nancy wailed, her fingers clutching the blue gingham fabric as if it were a lifeline. Jack helped her straighten the small garment out over the table.

"Is it Carly's?"

Carly's dad nodded, pointing to a small flower on the bodice. "Nancy embroidered that. A primrose. Carly constantly plucked them from the side of the stream." He looked from Tyler, to Fletcher, to Dee, then back at the young chief. "Does this mean she's dead?"

Tyler shook his head. "Not necessarily. These were found recently and in places known mostly by the locals. We think it's more likely an indication she's about to be moved."

Jack straightened, his expression thoughtful. "Does this mean Carly may still be around here? Still alive? Still in the area with whoever—"

Nancy sat bolt upright, a blast of hope brightening her face. "Could that be true? This could mean she's still here, still alive?"

Tyler folded Nancy's hands in his. "Listen to me, both of you. I want to find Carly, too. Desperately want to find her. There may be a lot these sandals can tell us, but right now, we can't afford to jump to any kind of assumption about them. Please let us work through this, and we will get you any progress as we have it. Please."

"What about a door-to-door search?" Jack demanded. "If she's still in Mercer—"

Fletcher stepped closer to the table. "We can't without probable cause. It's illegal. Besides—" he cleared his throat and crossed his arms over his chest "—if the kidnapper has her hidden, a door-to-door search probably wouldn't turn up anything. It's truly unlikely one of your neighbors is keeping her in a spare bedroom. If someone has her hidden, a casual search won't reveal it."

Nancy seemed to deflate, her face taking on a more resigned look. Jack nodded.

Dee ached with a steady pain that seemed to radiate from her heart into every muscle and bone. More than a physical soreness of the attack, this intense craving grew from her desire to help as well as heal, expanding like a balloon about to explode. She burst from her chair so abruptly that Tyler and Fletcher stepped backward. Her words of pleading erupted from her. "Please. Can I talk to you? Back at your house. One parent to another. Please." She focused on Nancy. "One mother to another."

A heavy silence hung in the air a moment, then Tyler put his hand on her arm. "Dee. I don't think this is the time—"

"Yes." Nancy stood and came around the table, a determined look suddenly taking form in her eyes. She grabbed Dee's hands and pulled her close. "We have not done that. Talked to another parent about…Carly. Yes. Please come."

Dee ignored Tyler's scowl. "This afternoon?"

Jack stepped up behind Nancy, and his hand closed around her arms, supporting her. His low voice held a comforting rumble. "This afternoon would be fine." He turned to Tyler. "Please let us know if you find out anything else."

Tyler stood straighter. "Of course." He and Jack shook hands, then the young doctor guided his wife out of the office, his hand on her lower back.

Tyler swung toward Dee. "You promised me that—"

"I couldn't stand their pain any longer." She plunged on as he started to protest. "I've followed this in the papers, Tyler. Y'all are doing everything you can, but I might be able to help them. Them. Not the case. *Them.*"

Tyler did not relent. "He's a doctor."

"But not a therapist. He's a surgeon." Impulsively, Dee reached out and grabbed Tyler's hands, pulling him close. "Please listen to me. I'm not a therapist either, but I've been where they are. Even if I only listen and ask about Carly, my guess is that I'll be able to get them to talk to me in a way they haven't been able to talk to you. Remember what she said about the star?"

Tyler nodded, his face still stoic.

Dee took a deep breath. "I want to talk to her about Carly dancing in their den, about how her breath smelled as a baby." She paused. "About how the emptiness of losing your only child is like a sinkhole in your heart that can't be filled by any other thing, any other person." She stepped back and looked at both of them. She had to convince them. "Have either of you talked about Carly as a little girl, not just another missing kid case?"

Tyler grabbed her arms in an explosive move that startled both her and Fletcher. His low, almost breathless words, froze Dee in place. "Don't ever…*ever* doubt how hard we've tried to find Carly. Ever." Releasing her, Tyler turned and left the room.

Stunned, Dee looked at Fletcher. "What did I do?"

Fletcher's enigmatic gaze betrayed nothing about how he felt. He simply took a deep breath and said, "Too many people mistake calmness for a lack of passion. You questioned who he is as a man as well as a cop. He doesn't need that right now." With that, he left her alone in the room.

Tears fuzzed Dee's vision, and she crossed her arms tightly. Tyler was the last person she'd want to hurt, and she'd blundered horribly by not seeing how much he had invested in the attempt to find Carly. She just wanted to help!

Dee slowly walked from the interrogation room to the door of Tyler's office. His back was toward her, but she could tell he stared at something in his hand. A photo. He gently replaced it on his phone, and Dee thought her heart would burst. A photo of Carly.

She inhaled deeply, shuddering. "Tyler…I'm sorry."

He stood quietly a moment, then turned. "No." His soft words focused on her. "No. I'm the one who should be sorry. I should not lose control. It's just that—" He broke off, glancing at the photo again.

"It's Carly."

He nodded.

Dee stepped into his office and shut the door. The click of the latch made him turn to face her, his blue eyes dark with concern.

"It's a passion we both share." She crossed to stand beside him, not entirely sure of what she meant to say, but the words seemed to tumble out on their own. "I don't know what this has done to me, Tyler, this finding of Carly's shoes. Seeing Nancy and Jack like that. It's like something has been set afire here." She clasped her hands just above her stomach and pressed in on her diaphragm. "I ache. It's like a craving to help them."

"Maybe it's God."

His low words stunned her, and she stepped back. He couldn't mean…"What?"

He glanced down at his desk for a moment, as if he would find the right words written on its top, then back at her. "God guides us in all sorts of ways, Dee."

A darkness clouded the back of her mind. "God left me three years ago. This has nothing to do with Him."

Tyler looked her over carefully, as if trying to search her soul, then lifted one shoulder in resignation. "Be careful with Nancy."

Dee nodded and squared her shoulders, determined to return to the reason she came to his office, more than to apologize. "Have you talked to Jack alone at all?"

He shook his head. "They never let go of each other. Haven't since the day Carly disappeared. We should have interviewed them apart, but a neighbor saw Carly going into the woods with the dog so they were never really suspects. I didn't push it. Nancy sort of collapses when Jack steps away, as if she's terrified he'll leave, too."

"I doubt it."

Tyler's expression snapped back into cop mode, stoic but questioning. "I beg your pardon."

Dee stepped closer. "It's not about abandonment. It's about support." As his look grew more questioning, she continued, reaching to take his hands in hers. As her fingers closed over his, she realized that she wanted to comfort more than the Bradfords.

She wanted Tyler to feel as safe with her as she did with him. She squeezed his fingers. "It's not about losing Jack. It's about being alone. Alone with your thoughts. That's when your imagination runs wild. And that's going to happen now. Anyone who reads a paper knows that when a child is taken and not killed right away, then the motive may be something even…worse. If Nancy doesn't think it, Jack will, and it'll make both of them crazy."

He tensed but didn't pull away. She stepped closer, turning her face up to his. "When something like this happens, the last thing you want is to be alone, even for a minute. Your mind goes insane with thoughts about the ones missing." She blinked hard as sudden memories of Joshua and Mickey splashed in her mind, then took a deep breath. "You have flashbacks, and your arms ache to hold them. You have to hold *something* or you'll go truly nuts. That's why she clings to him. Her arms want her daughter, but Carly is *just not there*."

He cleared his throat, his eyes bright. "Where are you going with this?"

"Come with me. Let's do this together. You're the law, you know the details and can put the pieces together. I'm a mom, I can hear their hearts. I can give you *more* pieces, *more* insights for the puzzle. If I can get Nancy to talk to me alone, sit with me, mother-to-mother, Jack might be ready to talk to you, man-to-man. He's *got* to be feeling things he hasn't dared share with his wife."

"How do you know that?"

Her mouth twisted with a touch of amusement. "Because he's a man. You guys have this amazing, sometimes maddening instinct to protect those you love, and he probably has had thoughts, maybe even suspicions that he can't share with her because he knows they'll frighten her. Likewise, Nancy may have held back things from him she'd share with another woman. Between the two of them, they may know stuff they don't know they know. Y'know?"

One corner of Tyler's mouth jerked as if he were fighting a smile. "Which is a key to most investigations."

She dropped his hands and held her arms wide. "See? Maybe I can help." She dropped them to her side. "Please?"

Again, he considered her a moment, then reached for his hat. "First, I need to get the dress and sandals out of the room and get Wayne started on the forensics. We're not going to take any chances with this. We'll get lunch, then I want to go back to where you were attacked. That will give Nancy and Jack time to pull their thoughts together, to recover from finding out their daughter may still be alive."

Today was a "nice" day. Her captor was in a good mood and the air had been filled with tuneless whistles and hums all morning.

Carly picked morosely at her breakfast plate as the eggs congealed and the scent of the bacon grew bitter. Last night she'd read in one of her books how the villain had tricked the heroine into taking poison that had been hidden in her food. Her food looked okay, but with villains, you never could tell.

She looked at her captor through lowered eyelashes. Across the room, more toys had appeared, and the villain in Carly's life was making sure a hand-held DVD player had the right batteries. A stack of new

DVDs had joined the books on the shelves, pulled with glee from a large paper sack on the floor.

The whistling paused. "Sweetheart?"

Carly cringed at the word. "What?"

A hand rested on the stack of DVD cases. "Let me know what you think of these. I don't want you to get bored."

"Then let me go home."

Immediately, Carly froze. She hadn't meant to say it. It was exactly the kind of thing she'd learned *not* to say in the first few days here, the kind of sentence that caused her captor to flip suddenly from nice to horrible.

The hand on the DVDs trembled slightly, then Carly's villain rushed at her, eyes wide with anger.

Carly screamed and scrambled backward on the bed, causing the breakfast tray to slip off the bed and scatter eggs, bacon, and fruit all over the floor, where pounding feet crushed it into the rug. Carly pressed herself against the wall, but clawlike fingers curled around her arms, jerking her forward. A sickly sweet scent washed over her as the shouted words hurt her ears.

"You *are* home!"

Her captor flung her sideways and Carly hit the headboard, then sank down on the bed, pulling her pillow tightly against her. The room went silent as the door slammed and the lock clicked.

Her arm throbbed from the blow against the padded headboard, and unstoppable tears stung her eyes. Carly hugged her pillow and rolled toward the wall, drawing her knees up to her chest.

"Please, Lord," she whispered. "Where are You?"

EIGHT

The Federal Café's daily special—lasagna, garlic bread, drink and a dessert of steaming peach cobbler—sat enticingly in front of both of them. Dee waited as Tyler lowered his head in a silent grace before the meal, ignoring the urge to join him. Then both attacked the food with the relish of two people who had not bothered with breakfast.

He paused to take a sip of water. "Do you like Italian?"

"I make my own spaghetti sauce." Dee grinned at his look of disbelief. "Seriously. My mother-in-law taught me. She was Italian, and every inch the stereotypical Italian mom. She loved to feed her men, and she guilted me into learning how to make the sauce. We'd make it by the gallons twice a year and freeze it in plastic bags."

Tyler reached for another slice of bread. "I bet it's delicious."

"Much better than anything you can buy, I can promise you." Dee paused, her thoughts drifting back more than a decade. "I resented it at first, this idea that she was making me learn to cook something you could buy so easily. The sauce in the jars is not all that bad.

Then I started to enjoy it. Not just the cooking for Mickey and Joshua but the act of cooking itself. I realized that cooking and chemistry have a lot in common, and I always loved chemistry in high school. What about you? Do you cook much?"

"I'm more into sandwiches and instant oatmeal. You'd get lost in my kitchen. It's big and there's almost nothing in it." He shifted a bit in his chair, then took another bite of the pasta. "Of course, if you truly tried to cook in there, you'd scare Patty half to death."

An odd twinge of jealousy tickled the back of Dee's mind. "Patty?"

He looked up at her. "All these lunches, and I haven't mentioned Patty?"

A girlfriend? Tyler never struck her as the type who would live with…. "Nope, you've never mentioned Patty before." She swallowed hard and tried to make her voice sound casual. "Is she your girlfriend?"

Tyler froze, then his eyes glittered with a teasing expression. "You aren't jealous of Patty, are you?"

She shrugged and pressed the tines of her fork deep into the lasagna, trying to look nonchalant, but the heat in her cheeks told her she wasn't succeeding. "No. Of course not. I just wondered."

"Patty is my dog." His grin broadened. "Although I'm flattered you thought otherwise."

"I didn't think—" Her gaze met his, and she blushed even harder when she saw the gleam in his eyes. "Stop that. You, sir, are running the risk of getting pasta dumped on your head."

He laughed. A good sound, she thought, one she hadn't quite heard enough of lately. "What kind of dog?"

"A peekapoo. Half poodle, half Pekinese. Although I think the 'poo' part was a toy poodle, maybe even a standard, not the typical miniature. Patty's more than twenty pounds of energy. Definitely not a lap dog."

"Why Patty?"

"For the New England Patriots mascot."

"You like football?"

It was his turn to shrug. "I enjoy the game, but I didn't name her. She came with the house I bought because the owner couldn't keep her at his new residence. He, on the other hand, was a major fan. He also had a tomcat named Brady, but he gave that to his daughter."

"I'll have to meet her. I could break in the kitchen with some homemade dog treats. That might win her over."

He motioned to Laurie to bring the check. "I don't know. I'd definitely have to introduce you to her slowly. She's always been jealous of other women in the house."

"I don't blame her."

Tyler's eyes widened, and Dee wondered if he'd notice if she slid under the table. The words were just out before she could stop them. Now her face felt as if it were on fire. *Why did I say that!*

Out of the corner of her eye, Dee saw Laurie approaching and almost leaped from her chair. "Look! Here's the check!" She dug into her jeans pocket for her cash.

Tyler chewed his lower lip, his eyes glinting with ill-disguised humor. He held out his hand. "I'll get it."

"That's not nec—"

"It'll be a business lunch. We are working on a case."

She withdrew her hand from her pocket. "Oh. Okay, then."

He took the check from a grinning Laurie, who wished them a good afternoon, then they headed for the register near the door. After Tyler paid, he escorted her to his cruiser and held the door for her.

Dee settled into the front seat, her eyes taking in each piece of equipment. As he got in, she gingerly touched the radio. "This is the first time I've ever been in a police car. At least in the front."

His hand paused on the way to the ignition, and he looked at her askance. "You've spent a lot of the time in the *backseat* of police cars, have you?"

Dee's eyes widened, and a sound that was half choke, half nervous laughter burst from her throat. "No! I mean, not like that—" Frustrated, she forced herself to stop, recoup, and face him. "How do you do that to me?"

Tyler started the car. "Do what?"

"Find holes in my sentences big enough to drive humor through."

He put the car in reverse and backed out of his parking space. "I don't think it's me. You're usually pretty precise with what you say. Maybe you've just gotten comfortable enough with me to drop your guard."

She pressed her back against the seat. "Y'know, for a small-town cop, you're pretty clever."

"I watch a lot of television."

Dee laughed.

"Ah, now that's a sound I like. You don't do that enough."

The compliment sent a tinge of shyness through her,

especially as she recalled her thoughts about his recent burst of laughter. "Neither do you."

Now it was his turn to look a little uncomfortable, and after a few moments of silence, Tyler cleared his throat. "You know what we're about to do won't be easy, right?"

Tyler glanced at Dee, trying to gauge her thoughts. When he'd suggested going back to the attack site earlier, she'd barely registered his words, and that worried him. Taking a victim back to the scene of a crime could be risky, but he wanted to find out if she could remember anything more about her attacker. His plan—lunch, then the site—had been geared toward putting her at ease. He just hoped it would work.

Dee stared forward, quiet for a moment. She nodded once, then remained silent for the rest of the short ride, the playful mood between them a memory lost in thin air. Tyler hated that, hated to see her go so somber, and he realized how thrilled he'd been at her laughter, her momentary jealousy.

Don't get distracted, he scolded himself. *This is about Carly, not how you feel about Dee.* Tyler took a deep breath and let it out slowly as he eased the cruiser to a stop, letting it drift to a halt on the shoulder opposite where he'd almost hit her. He flipped on the flashing lights to warn any approaching cars, then got out.

Dee followed him across the road, pausing to look down the steep embankment she'd clambered up the day before. Her gaze grew distant, and she swayed a bit.

Tyler took her arm, his voice low. "Tell me again. How did it start?"

"I had just realized that the sandals were Carly's. Then I heard a voice demand I drop the shoes."

Tyler's words became a whisper. "Were those the exact words?"

She nodded, closing her eyes. "Drop the shoes."

"What did the voice sound like?"

Dee hesitated, tilting her head to one side, as if listening. "Gravelly. Hoarse."

"Hoarse, like they were sick?"

She shook her head, her eyes still closed. "Like they were trying not to sound normal. Like you'd make the voice of a monster if you were reading to a child."

Tyler watched her. Interesting comparison. And very apt, if the attacker were trying to disguise his voice. Dee seemed very into the memory now, and she swayed again. Tyler wrapped his arm around her waist to steady her. "You ran."

Another nod. "I'm not a good runner. I knew I'd have a better chance in the woods than the path. To get here, to this road, to find help." She opened her eyes and looked up at him. "To find you." An odd light of recognition came into her eyes. "My first thought was to find you."

Tyler's chest tightened around his heart, but his brain came to the rescue. *The attacker. Focus on the attacker.* "Did he say anything else?"

Dee shook her head, still looking at him, then paused. She looked away into the woods. "He called me stupid. 'Stupid woman.'" Her gaze grew distant again. "And I think he was right-handed. He kept grabbing for the sandals with his right hand." She shrugged and looked down at the ground. "Not that *that* helps you any."

Tyler wanted to reassure her, to keep her in the memory. "You never know what tidbit will help. Do you remember anything else. A smell? You said the attacker was wearing a sweat suit?"

She nodded. "Really ratty. Like you'd wear to work on your car, not out to jog or see anyone. With a hood pulled down low over his face. I never saw a face." She frowned. "And I fell into a bed of purple wildflowers. That's the only scent I can remember."

"Tall? Short?"

She tilted her head again. "That I can't say. Taller than me, but most of the adults on the planet are." She paused again. "But skinny. Really skinny."

Now for the hard part. "Do you think you can walk back through it?"

She shook her head.

"I know it'll be hard—"

"No, it's not that." She reached a hand out toward the woods. "Tyler, I was running blind. All I could think about was getting around the next tree, getting more distance between us. I *might* be able to find that patch of flowers, but other than that I couldn't find that trail with a bloodhound—"

She stopped, turning on him suddenly, her eyes wide. "I hit him." She closed her hand tight on his arm. "I kicked him, too. Here." She placed her palm against his lower ribs, causing Tyler to stand a bit straighter. "I'm sure hard enough to leave a bruise. And here." She touched his jaw. "I'm positive I landed a good right cross, but low. Jawline or neck. Enough to push him backward. If we find someone soon, there might be bruises."

Soon. If only. Tyler fought to keep his mood level. In three months there had been no "soon." *From her mouth to Your ear, Lord.*

* * *

Dee felt her good mood waning as soon as they left the site and headed toward the Bradfords. The information she'd offered Tyler had been so minor. Tidbits, really. What could he possibly do with those? *What in the world made me think I could help him? Help Jack and Nancy, yes, but Tyler?* Her shoulders drooped and they both fell silent until they had passed back through Mercer on the way to Jack and Nancy Bradford's home.

"What is your goal in talking with Jack and Nancy?"

Dee hesitated at the abrupt question, then turned to gaze out the window, her thoughts drifting back over the past three years. "You can't imagine how lonely this is for them. It's not like being a couple who've never had children. They will never be that again. They've lost something that's a precious part of their very being, and each day is a painful journey through a kind of limbo. Your friends, no matter how much they love you, eventually burn out. They aren't experiencing your grief, so they fade away, tired of it. They *want* to keep on with you, but spiritually, emotionally, they can't. They have their own lives and families."

She looked down at her hands a moment, then continued. "When Joshua and Mickey were killed, I lost every desire to live. Every other thing in my life, even good ones like my parents and my work, were like ash. My faith vanished as thoroughly as fog on a summer morning. I still can't think of God as a provider, only as a taker. He took everything, then left."

She paused and looked out the window, wishing the peaceful springtime New Hampshire landscape could help her gather her thoughts and ease the restlessness in her mind. "Almost everyone leaves, eventually. I sank so fast…." She shook that thought away. "Aaron Jackson stayed near me almost three weeks. He called or e-mailed every day, just to ask me if I'd made it through the day in one piece. He sent me this book about a family who had lost their son. He pestered me until I read it, especially the part about deciding just to make it through today. Not tomorrow. Not forever. Just today. Every day was a decision. I can live without them today."

Dee glanced at Tyler, whose face remained stoic, his eyes focused on the road. "Go on," he whispered.

Looking back down at her lap, Dee forced herself to continue. "You see, that was huge. A huge daily decision because I didn't *want* to live without them, Tyler. I couldn't envision a life without them. Everything else— my parents, my work, everything—turned to smoke, something I could see but couldn't feel. Aaron pushed back, hung with me. He was a thousand miles away, but was the one who really got me through the toughest times."

She looked up at him again. "It's not that I want to be an Aaron for them—I'm not as strong as Aaron, and their grief is not my grief." She shrugged. "At least not yet." When he stiffened, she added, "And I hope not ever. But I can listen in a way few other people can."

Silence held reign in the car for a few moments, then Tyler spoke, his voice so low, she could barely hear it. "I pray you can, too. More than I've been able to."

Dee turned to him, puzzled. "What are you talking about? You've been awesome. Your whole team has." She twisted to her left until the seatbelt pressed into her hip and her body faced him. "I know I read Fletcher the riot act back there, and said some things to you that were unfair, but that's because I'm a mom who knows how bad they hurt!

"You were right, and I've been thinking about it since you said it. I've followed the press. I've listened to Fletcher talk to Maggie about the case. You've been handicapped from the beginning by the lack of evidence, the rain, the fact that you couldn't prove Carly had not run away. I can't imagine you doing more than you have. Just because you don't have the resources of the FBI or a big city force doesn't mean you haven't done everything that could be done. You care!" She flopped back to face forward again. "And that's a lot more than I can say about some cops in cases like this."

Tyler remained silent again, and she sneaked a glance at his face, to find him grinning. "You think this is funny?"

He shook his head. "I'm just glad you're on my side. I like your passion."

Dee crossed her arms, fighting her own smile. "Yeah, well, I'm glad I'm on your side as well."

Tyler's eyes widened a bit, but he said nothing as he turned into the long drive leading to the Bradfords' spacious and comfortable home. The half-timber Tudor home had been built almost sixty years ago, one of the first homes in a neighborhood that ran along Mercer's wide stream and catered mostly to professionals who made their money in Portsmouth, Manchester or Boston, then retreated in the evenings to Mercer's peaceful and secure small-town life. The large homes, mostly modeled on sister designs in Boston, rested on tree-clustered, pristinely manicured lawns.

Nancy Bradford opened the door herself, and she and Jack ushered Dee and Tyler into a cypress-lined foyer, Nancy's low kitten heels popping lightly on the Italian floor tiles. "I made tea and coffee, if you'd like some." She pointed to a door on the left side of the foyer. "It's in the library."

Taking a deep breath, Dee plunged in head first. "Actually, I was wondering if you and I could talk in Carly's room."

Nancy and Jack looked at each other, their discomfort shining on their faces. Before they could protest, Tyler placed his weight on both feet, focusing on Jack. "I could use some of that coffee, if you don't mind, Jack."

His "cop" stance, thought Dee, intrigued by how fast he'd slipped into a "divide and conquer" mode with her.

Jack looked from Tyler, to Nancy, to Dee, then back to his wife again, as if deciding his best course of action. Nancy pointed at the curving staircase at the end of the foyer. "Carly's room is this way, upstairs."

Jack, looking amazed and greatly relieved, motioned for Tyler to follow him, and the two men disappeared into the library. Dee followed Nancy's graceful ascent of the stairs, marveling at how clean the house was, how the aroma of vanilla and lavender lingered in the air both cleansing it and creating a calming ambience. After Mickey and Joshua died, her house had become a pig sty that worsened in exponential ways until her parents moved her into theirs, then cleaned and sold hers.

Carly's room didn't have the same scrubbed feel, although it reminded Dee distinctly of a design magazine's idea of what a little girl's room should look like. Pale yellow walls were accented with white shelves, holding neat lines of soft dolls, collectable plates, and Barbies still in their boxes. The closet doors had been removed, and the walls had been extended inward a foot or so, and the area had been converted into a combination closet, computer station and DVD setup. Children's books lined two of the closet shelves. On the smoothly made bed, a golden yellow comforter awaited Carly, the plump yellow and white pillows resting against the headboard.

Against the far wall and under a bay window, however, the real play area took shape, hidden from the doorway's line of sight. Baskets filled with well-loved and slightly soiled toys lined up on the edge of a soft, colorful rug, and a doll house crammed with furniture and small figurines sat near the head of the bed. On the seat of the bay window, a small white poodle lay, his head on his paws. When he saw Nancy, he raised his head expectantly, his tail beating a steady rhythm.

"Sasha," Nancy said, her voice almost a whisper. "He's been here since Carly disappeared. Jack has to physically carry him downstairs to eat and go out. He won't go on his own. And when he comes back in, he heads straight here." Now her voice dropped lower than a whisper. "It's killing me."

Nodding, Dee sat next to the loyal pooch, stroking his head. "I had to give Joshua's dog to a friend with boys. He was grieving himself to death, the same as I was, and we couldn't help each other."

A box of art supplies peeked from under the golden dust ruffle, and Dee pointed at it and looked up at Nancy. "Do you mind?"

Carly's mom shook her head and knelt to pull the box free of the bed, revealing a stack of drawings, crayons, chalks and watercolors. Art papers were covered with broad splashes of reds, greens, blues and yellows. Most of them were landscapes that overflowed with trees, the stream that danced through the backyard, and oversized butterflies.

Nancy touched them lovingly. "Carly loves butterflies. She drew them incessantly. One of the teachers at the school raises butterflies, and he promised he'd teach her when she got old enough."

"Will she have him next year?"

"No. He's not actually one of *her* teachers. He just saw her butterflies on a school art display and asked her at lunch one day."

Nancy handed the drawings up to Dee, who examined each one carefully. "Translating art into science." Dee traced one of the butterflies with her fingers. "Is she interested in science?"

"Not that I know of. She likes the woods." Nancy sat on the bay seat next to Dee and pulled Sasha into her lap. The dog sniffed her hands, then nuzzled one palm. Nancy scratched him behind the ears and under the chin, and the dog sighed heavily and nestled down against her stomach. "She'd sit here with Sasha for hours reading, or drawing what she sees out the window. Somewhere in that box are drawings of snow falls, thunderstorms and spring flowers. Sometimes, she would go out into the woods, then come back and draw a flower or lichen she'd found."

"More art than science."

Nancy nodded, then shrugged. "Jack hopes it's more biology or botany than art. He had wanted a boy, wanted to have another doctor in the family. He comes from a long line of surgeons and families with all boys. Carly is the first girl in two generations. I thought he'd be disappointed, but he fell in love with her the minute he saw her." She smiled wryly. "Still hopes she'll be a doctor, though. So he was thrilled with the idea that she'd learned to raise butterflies. Saw it as her first scientific curiosity."

"Have you met this teacher?"

Nancy's finely arched brows came together over thoughtful dark eyes. "I think we met him at a parents' meeting once. Sweet man. Mr. Riley."

Dee scanned the room again. "Does Carly play with all these dolls?"

Nancy chuckled, a soft sound that surprised and pleased Dee. "No. Most of these are mine. The books, too. They were in storage until we bought this house, then Carly asked if they could be put in here. She says they remind her of how much I love her and how much my mama loves me." She paused. "Mahmaam. That's what Carly calls my mother. Not sure where she gets it."

Dee paged through more of the drawings, amazed at the maturity in the artwork. Carly had picked up the technique of adding shadows for depth and altering shapes and sizes for perspective. Then, she peeled away another page, revealing a dark, starkly different drawing. Flattened, without the depths of the other, this one depicted what looked like a hospital E.R., with a black-haired little girl on the examining table, her foot encased in a cast. The nurse standing next to her had bright red hair, and her mouth was open as if in a scream, and her eyes wide and green. Carly had drawn lightning strikes emanating from the nurse.

Dee looked up at Nancy in alarm. "What is this?"

The cloud of sadness settled again over Nancy as she

reached for the drawing. "We're not sure. Six months ago, Carly broke her ankle. We took her to the E.R. in Portsmouth, and they fixed her up. While we waited for the paperwork, I went to the ladies' room, leaving Carly alone for less than five minutes. When I came back, she was in tears, saying a nurse had come in and yelled at her, telling her that her father was a bad man, that she should hope he never had to set her leg."

"My goodness. What happened?"

"I demanded to know who had said such a thing. They declared that no nurse had been in the room." Nancy sighed. "We asked her to draw it, and the red hair told us it was probably Bethany Davidson. She's a nurse there and the only person to ever file a complaint against Jack with the AMA. She claims he let her niece die on the operating table."

"Did they fire her?"

Nancy handed her the artwork. "No. They could never prove she was there. She wasn't on the schedule. They even pulled surveillance tapes at Jack's insistence, but Davidson wasn't on any of them."

Dee stared at her. "An eight-year-old doesn't make something like that up. Especially not with the detail of red hair."

"No. But it becomes the word of a trusted, experienced nurse with an alibi against a frightened child's."

"Did Tyler question this nurse?" Dee returned the disturbing picture to its box.

Nancy nodded. "Twice, if I remember. Once alone, and once with that FBI agent who worked on the case. Davidson claims she was out of town."

Dee slipped off the window seat and sat on the floor, pushing the art box back under the bed. In doing so, her hand brushed up against leather, and she pulled out a stray shoe, a small leather Mary Jane with a silver buckle. Nancy gasped and pulled it from Dee's grasp. Tears filled her eyes but did not escape. "This has been lost for months! I wanted her to wear them to church one Sunday, but she could only find one."

Dee smiled, remembering Joshua's adventures with his shoes. "My son once lost a pair at a state fair, one at time. And he was forever leaving them in some neighbor's yard." She watched as Nancy's quivering fingers traced the strap. "What was her favorite store?"

Nancy placed the shoe in her lap, and Sasha sniffed it thoroughly, as if Carly's foot would suddenly reappear in it. "There's a pet store in Portsmouth that she likes. She made friends with all the clerks and the dog trainer. Carly wasn't very girly." She smiled sadly and looked around the room. "This is mostly me. I keep hoping she'll suddenly turn into a frou-frou girl, I guess. I imagine one day she'll wake up and ask if she can have her own room with her own interests. I've asked, but she insists she likes it like this."

"Enjoy it," Dee said. "Independence comes way too soon for most of us moms." Her heart swelled when Nancy smiled at her.

"You really think Carly will come home, don't you?"

Without knowing why, Dee suddenly realized that she really did think the little girl who loves butterflies was still alive. "I do. Seriously."

Nancy took a deep breath. "Tell me about Joshua."

Dee braced her back against the side wall of the bay seat and gathered her thoughts about her son. She also made a mental note to ask Tyler about the pet store and the mysterious Mr. Riley, the grown man who'd expressed such an unusual interest in one particular little girl.

NINE

Tyler let Dee take the lead on this, realizing that Nancy's vulnerability made her the more fragile of the two; he could talk to Jack until the women finished. Jack, on his part, had appeared eager for male companionship. He'd eagerly dived into the chat, and so far they had talked sports over the coffee, then Jack had invited him to the backyard. They simply strolled a few moments, then Tyler realized that they were slowly heading for the spot where Jack had watched Carly vanish into the woods with Sasha, never to be seen again. Time to break the ice.

"How's Nancy really doing?"

Jack's noncommittal shrug told him nothing. "She's still shaken, as you can imagine. Sometimes I'm absolutely terrified to leave her."

"What about you? How are you handling it?" He paused. "Honestly."

Jack walked in silence a few moments. "I'd be better if I could do something. *Anything*. I love Nancy, but staying here and waiting for Carly to suddenly reappear out of the trees is slowly making me crazy."

"Any new thoughts about anyone we should talk to?

Any other folks come to mind that might have had a problem with you or Nancy?"

Jack shook his head. "I've run myself ragged with that one. I've gone through every file I had here, had my office folks go through the files there and at the hospital. I called the AMA to see if they'd forgotten to notify me about anything. Bethany Davidson's name came up again."

"But we've talked to her. Anyone else?"

Jack paused, staring out into the woods. "One of the women in my office reminded me of the Titlebaum lawsuit."

Tyler straightened with renewed curiosity. "You're being sued?"

Jack shook his head, still looking toward the trees. "I'm suing him for patent infringement over an instrument I created that Dr. Titlebaum claims he invented independent of my work." Without pausing for breath, Jack detailed the instrument's function and the operations that led to the need for it.

Tyler absorbed the technical language without understanding. "That sounds like a professional dispute. Do you truly think he'd respond by kidnapping your child?"

Crossing his arms, Jack dropped his gaze to the ground. "Not until the countersuit he filed is settled." He cleared his throat and finally looked back at Tyler. "You know we're still having trouble imagining that anyone who *knows* us would do this. Nancy still can't accept it, but I'm beginning to doubt it's random. What about you?"

"I honestly don't know, Jack. I've seen some odd things, but even I would hate to admit this is someone we've been around every day of our lives." Tyler took a deep breath and plunged on as they turned and headed back toward the house. "Anyone new who showed interest in Carly?"

Again, the shake. "We protected her as best we could, Tyler." He paused and his voice cracked. "I really miss her."

Tyler crossed his arms and stopped, facing Jack. "Any chance you can go back to work if someone else stayed with Nancy? I know it's going to be hard, but you can't put your life on hold much longer. Eventually, you need to take care of yourself as well as Nancy. Nancy loves you with all her heart, Jack. She has to know you can't stay at the house much longer. That you need to work, have a goal."

Jack stared at Tyler a long time, his face unmoving, his eyes unreadable. Then he continued walking. "I've thought about calling her mother."

"Do it."

Jack nodded, and, after a few more moments of silence, asked Tyler a question about the Red Sox. With a wry grin, Tyler answered him, letting the subject drift back to sports.

When they got back to the house, the women waited in the library, and Nancy let out a full-bodied laugh as Dee finished the last words of a story. Jack stared, stunned, and Tyler nudged him forward, whispering, "Ask now."

"When you're gone," Jack whispered back, and Tyler dropped it. Jack was probably right on that one, but he did step forward and greet his wife with a kiss and a squeeze on her arm. "Everything okay?"

Nancy returned the kiss. "Absolutely. Dee is a delight to talk to."

Jack turned to Dee, his eyes gleaming with pleasure. "Then you'll have to come back more often."

Dee gave Nancy a quick hug. "I will. Promise." She paused, a touch of concern on her face. "And you're positive about the articles?"

Nancy nodded. "I think they will help."

"I'll send them to you first for approval."

"Thank you."

Tyler and Dee backed away from the couple then turned toward the door as they exchanged final goodbyes and thank-yous. Tyler held the car door for Dee, and she settled in as if she belonged there, a look of true satisfaction on her face.

Tyler turned the cruiser back toward the office, and they were clear of the Bradfords' drive before he spoke, even though his curiosity ate a hole in him.

"Okay, what articles?"

A broad, gleeful grin spread over Dee's face. "I wondered how long you'd wait to ask. I'm going to propose a series of articles about the Bradfords to the local newspaper editors. Up-close-and-personal follow-ups. With all the press this case has gotten, one of them should snap up the idea. Nancy and I think they might help the search, or at least keep folks' minds on Carly." She cast a sideways glance at him. "Do you mind if I quote you?"

Tyler hesitated. He couldn't decide if this was way out of line or if Dee had stumbled on a path of healing for herself as well as Nancy. He looked deep into his own instincts but found no immediate negative reaction to the idea. In fact, something far inside told him this might help Dee more than Nancy. Still, her closeness to him held its own kind of dangers. "Just tell me what you're quoting. And no case details. As you know, we're holding some things back on purpose."

She held up her right hand in a scout salute. "Promise. But…speaking of case details…"

Now his gut gave a twist of dread. "What case details?"

Dee turned a bit sideways within the confines of the seat belt. "You've talked to Bethany Davidson, right?"

"Twice. Nancy told you about Davidson?"

"Yep. Did she tell you that Carly drew a picture of a redheaded nurse screaming at her in the E.R.?"

Tyler knew his surprise showed all over his face. "How did you find that out?"

"We went through Carly's artwork. Very revealing. So, do you mind if I interview Davidson for one of the articles?"

Right at that moment, he had the urge to put a lid on the whole article idea. *This could get much worse.* He took a deep breath. "Dee, as much as I appreciate your help, I need you to be careful. Anything, *anything* could turn up a lead…or drive the kidnapper deeper into hiding. Maybe I should go with you."

"I understand, Tyler, I really do. And I promise I'll be careful. But you being there will hamper her honesty. She might tell me something she'd never say in front of a cop. Anything I hear that appears suspicious, I'll let you know. So can I talk to Davidson?"

He raised a shoulder in a half shrug. Technically he couldn't really stop her.

After a moment, Dee cleared her throat. "Or…you could go with me, wait somewhere." Dee flopped back in the seat to face forward again, satisfied. "Then we could go talk to Mr. Riley and the pet store folks."

An alarm bell went off in the back of Tyler's head, and that slight feeling of dread escalated. "Who's Mr. Riley? And what pet store?"

Color drained from Dee's face. "A teacher at Carly's school who showed a real interest in her artwork, promised to teach her to raise butterflies. The pet store was her favorite place in Portsmouth. She made friends with all the employees so they'd let her pet the kittens and puppies."

Now Tyler felt the heat leave his own face. "We'll be back in the station in five minutes. I want to hear everything you and Nancy discussed."

Two tears slid down Carly's cheeks as another long lock of her ebony hair hit the starkly white sheet draped around her neck. Since this whole process had started, she'd counted the curls as they fell. Thirty-five so far. She reached up to brush the tears away.

"Don't move. And stop whimpering. It's just hair. It'll grow."

"But my hair has never been cut. Mama said—"

Hands clamped down on her shoulders, cutting off her words. The handle of the scissors, still clutched in her captor's right hand, dug into her collar bone, and the tips of the blades spread menacingly against her cheek. "This is your own fault. If you hadn't lost the sandals, they wouldn't have started looking again. The Bradfords, oh high-and-so-mighty Doctor Jack, they think you're theirs. Their little girl. Well, they can look all they want for a little girl. What they won't be looking for is a boy."

Carly's lips tightened. "I'm not a boy."

"For now you will be. Until we can get you out of reach, you will be."

Carly sniffed and tried to blink away the rest of her tears. She looked up toward the window. *Please,* she prayed. *Please send someone soon.*

TEN

Dee stared out the window of her cabin into the dense New Hampshire woods, her mind wandering as wild and free as an animal in that thick undergrowth. The woods enchanted her as nothing else could, and the fact that the retreat sat so isolated and away from the world had been the only reason she'd agreed to come. What no one alive knew was that Aaron Jackson had begged her to come before his death. He knew these rolling hills and lush forest would help her heal. She had finally agreed to come as a tribute to him.

Aaron had been right. Slowly, gradually, she was healing.

Dee's mind flashed on Tyler, who had driven her back to the retreat this afternoon and walked her to the door, his hand warm and comforting on her arm. Their growing friendship had been a part of that healing, almost from the moment they had met. His nonstop curiosity about her and her life, his willingness to be gentle and open when they talked had charmed her. Still, something had clicked inside today, when she had snapped to his defense, when his touch on her arm made her trip over her tongue.

Am I falling for him? She sat straighter, ignoring the blinking cursor on her computer.

Her eyes shifted to the left, to the open closet at the back of the cabin. The emerald green dress, her last gift from Mickey, still hung there, waiting for her to lose those last pounds. She had loved Mickey with all her heart, and life without him had felt impossible. She knew, on some level, that she would always love him, always hold him dear. She had made it through three years, and her thoughts no longer centered on him, but Mickey still lingered in the back of her mind.

Her thoughts turned more regularly toward Tyler these days, and she'd found herself idly wondering what he was doing at that moment, how his day had gone. Yet each time she did, a twinge of guilt tweaked at her conscience, as if she were cheating on her husband. Mild, but constant. Was she ready to move on—to date again? Maybe.

Joshua, however, was a different story. She continued to feel his absence as if she had a knife embedded in her heart, a knife that had twisted once again during her chat with Nancy, accentuating the sense of loss. Joshua would live forever in her mind and soul, forever eight, instead of growing to eleven, as he would be now. She should be contemplating his teen years, when he would be all raging hormones and gangly legs, instead of remembering his death.

A picture of them taken at a family reunion flashed through her mind, reminding her that Joshua looked more like her brother than Mickey, with his long blond hair instead of Mickey's half-Italian dark hair and eyes. Yet they would always be tied together in her mind and heart. Father and son.

I wonder what Tyler's kids will look like?

The abrupt thought so startled Dee that she burst from her chair and strode out on the porch, gulping in rich, fresh air. The breeze on her face felt like a cleansing bath, and she sighed, letting the wind and scents of pine and wildflowers wash over her.

Late spring in New Hampshire came with a flood of new life, and it surged all around the cabin, even in the fading light of evening. Near the edge of her porch, lavender blooms carpeted a wide swatch of the woodland floor, filling the entire area with a sweet smell, especially in the crisp air following a quick rain or the moist breezes of early dawn. The birch and oak trees, their limbs covered with new leaves, rustled with birds and squirrels settling for the night, while the pines whispered their soft evensong, one Dee knew well from back home.

Being here had brought a peace to her mind and soul like nothing before had. Finally, she had found within herself the hints of healing. She craved this now, wanting to embrace memories of Mickey and Joshua without the overlay of pain they always brought. That was still to come, but at least she no longer had to make a conscious, intentional decision to live through the day.

So would her growing friendship with Tyler help—or hinder? She tried to push away thoughts about Tyler, but one lingered. The last thing he'd said to her, on the porch of the retreat this afternoon, was "I think God is opening some doors in this case. I can feel it." His grin had been so boyish and excited, that she'd not said anything about the case—or God.

Dee turned her face toward the few bright patches of blue that shone through the tops of the trees. "You left," she whispered. "Why did You leave me?"

It was the first time she'd talked to God in three years.

Dee turned and went back in, her gaze falling briefly on the green dress again. So, no, maybe she wasn't ready for someone like Tyler, yet. *Yet.*

Brushing a tear away and trying to rein her thoughts in from the wild wanderings, she stared at the blinking cursor. The article, so close to completion, just needed its ending and a bit of editorial tweaking.

Dee grinned and leaned back in her chair. When she'd called the local paper's editor this afternoon, he'd been ballistically thrilled about the idea of her filing regular columns, especially about Carly's abduction. She was in a prime position to provide insights no one else had, and he wanted to see something that night. If she could get it to him before midnight, he'd run it the next day.

Although she'd been staying in the lodge house for safety after the attack, Dee had insisted on coming back to the privacy and silence of the cabin to write and handle her correspondence, and the remaining hours of the afternoon had been amazingly productive. She'd returned to the lodge for dinner, but was now back at the screen, taking advantage of the last hours of light, wanting to get even more done.

Taking a deep breath, Dee sank back into the article, typed the ending then verified her referenced Web sites and tightened the prose. Finally satisfied, she saved it, attached it to an e-mail and sent it off to the editor, with a copy to Nancy.

Dee stared at her e-mail account a moment, the in-comparable urge to share that most writers have not quite satisfied by the submission to the editor or the one sent to Nancy. Grinning, she typed a hurried note to her mother and sent the article off to her as well. Then, riding the same impulse, she composed a quick note to

Tyler, just suggesting that he make sure to check the paper the next morning.

With a deep, long sigh and sense of accomplishment, Dee closed her laptop, unplugged it, and tucked it under her arm. She locked the front door of her cabin and headed back to the lodge, feeling a lightness of heart and mind that she'd not felt in a long time.

Darkness had fully enclosed the retreat, and the small number of area lights did little to illuminate her way back to the lodge. She picked her way carefully along the trail, keeping the lights of the lodge house in sight. The night scents and sounds, enhanced by the light chill in the air, filled her senses, and suddenly Dee Kelley just felt profoundly glad to be alive.

She laughed, and gave a little skip forward, a burst of energy filling her body and mind. Another skip, and Dee felt as if she could hear the rush of blood through her veins, the sound of her own breaths filling her lungs. An unfamiliar charge of joy flowed over her, and she spun around in a light dance step. It was as if a casing of ice that had covered her, holding her prisoner, had now shattered, and a warmth of new life surged around her.

Dee skidded to a sudden halt, her eyes turning again to the sky. "Is this You?" She turned on the trail, yet continued to look upward. "Are *You* doing this?"

The crackling sound of shoes on dried leaves came from her left, and Dee spun, peering into the darkness. "Who's there?"

Only the natural sounds of insects and frogs responded at first, along with a light wind that stirred her hair around her face. Then she heard it again, more distinct this time and slightly ahead of her.

Dee glanced at the lodge house, not wanting to run,

but a flood of fear seized her and she broke into a trot, careful to clutch her computer close to her chest. She didn't stop, afraid of what she might hear next.

She arrived at the lodge and slowed, catching her breath. *You're just being paranoid. It was probably a rabbit or raccoon. Some night hunter.* In front of her, a welcoming glow blazed through the windows, showing some of the writers who had lingered long after dinner. Two of them hung out in the downstairs game room, playing air hockey. She climbed the steps of the back deck and looked inside, where one of the other women read by the fireplace, sipping tea. To her right, a yellow square on the ground showed that Maggie still worked in her office at the end of the hall, blinds wide open, as usual.

Normal. All was normal. With one glance back at the woods, Dee went inside, closed the door and locked it.

Tyler sat down hard in his office chair, ignoring the creaks of protest it gave off. He wrapped his hands around a hot mug of coffee and inhaled deeply, as if to start his absorption of caffeine before even taking a sip. He'd had another night of little sleep and odd dreams, most of which had to do with Carly and Dee in danger. He also couldn't get a midnight e-mail from Dee out of his head. It had simply said, "Made a connection. Maybe we can turn the press coverage to the good. Check the paper tomorrow."

"Whatever that means," he mumbled, stretching his legs out under his desk. He would be moving slow today, mind and body.

In fact, he'd just taken his first sip from the mug when his mother appeared in the door of his office, the local paper in hand and a pleased but curious look on her face. "You need to see this." Peg placed the paper, which had been folded open to page five, the op-ed page, on his desk and pointed.

He squinted a bit, then the letters came into focus. He stared down at the column headed with "One Parent's Journey."

Beneath the column head and Dee's byline, a black box contained a short editor's note.

Today we start a new column by local writer Dee Kelley, which will focus on cultural and newsworthy items within our community and how they may affect the way we raise our children. This first column deals with a recent event that concerns every parent in the area. Comments about Ms. Kelley's observations are welcome.

He scanned the column quickly, halfway afraid of what it would say, how much of the investigation Dee might reveal. A smile slowly spread over his face, however, then he read it again, more thoroughly this time.

The Hope of a Mother's Heart

Nancy Bradford feels lost in her own kitchen, and there's not a mother alive who would blame her. Her husband Jack wanders around in their backyard aimlessly, occasionally stopping to stare into the woods behind their home, eyes searching, heart aching.

Three months ago, Carly, Nancy and Jack's eight-year-old daughter, raced off to play with her dog in those woods. She never returned. The intense search for the missing girl involved local and state police as well as federal agents, but after a few weeks, the search dwindled as every clue led only to a dead end.

Yet hope never faded for Nancy and Jack, and the recent discovery of new leads has rekindled their anticipation that Carly will be found. Nancy shared that hope and anticipation with me recently, as we sat in Carly's bedroom, a sweet little girl's room filled with dolls and toys that feels too big and lonely these days.

"I miss the little things the most." In her lap, Nancy holds Sasha, the little poodle who misses Carly so much he stays in her bedroom all the time. "The sound of her flip-flops on the kitchen tile, her screams of joy when she played with Sasha. She used to plant this silly, wet kiss on me before school, just to see if she could mess up my makeup and make me fussy…"

The article went on to describe Dee's own loss, and it summarized what had been in the press so far about Carly and the steadily increasing numbers of children who are abducted every year. It asked people to scour their memories and to never forget about Carly Bradford. Related sources, including their Web sites and phone number, were listed in a sidebar to the article. Tyler sank into his chair, his forearms resting on the desk. "Good for you, Dee Kelley. Let's hope your little tribute triggers some memories and turns over some rocks." He looked at Carly's picture. "Hang in there, Carly. We're going to find you."

* * *

The empty boxes hit the concrete floor with a hollow thud, and Carly's captor placed a roll of packing tape on the bookcase. "Pack!" The brusque command had a terse finality to it, and the captor turned to leave.

Carly sat straighter on the bed. "Where are we going?"

Her villain stopped, then looked over a shoulder at her. "South. First I have to take care of that meddling witch once and for all. She's stirring up the entire town! Then we'll go where no one will find us. Pack!"

The door slammed and Carly stared at the boxes. "God," she whispered, "if we leave, Mama and Daddy will never come. No one will come." She slid off the bed and went to stare into the boxes. She sighed and put a few of the DVDs into one of the boxes. They were mostly boring anyway.

The books were different. Only two went into the box before the third one caught her eye. It was old, its binding cracked and pages yellow. But the beautiful, golden horse on the cover seemed real enough to stroke. She spoke the title aloud. *"Robin Kane—The Mystery of the Blue Pelican."*

Carly sat on the floor and scooted her back up against the case. "Maybe if I don't pack, we don't have to leave." She opened the cover, which cracked but held tight. The smell of old paper wafted around her, but Carly's gaze settled on the first sentence and she disappeared into the world of the young girl detective and her brilliant palomino, trying to ignore the curses and thuds echoing through the vent.

ELEVEN

Dee slowly replaced the cordless phone in its charger, still a little surprised by the answer she'd received. She turned to Maggie, who sat by the windows overlooking the front lawn, nursing a cup of tea. "Bethany Davidson has agreed to talk to me."

Maggie set the Earl Grey on a low table beside the chair. "Why does that surprise you? Didn't you call her and ask?"

Dee lifted a shoulder in a half shrug. "Maybe it shouldn't, but it does. And, yes, I did, after Tyler agreed to it. But I really expected her to say no. In a world of people who love Jack and Nancy Bradford, she stands out as the one who doesn't. She was one of Tyler's 'persons of interest' in this case. They interviewed her twice. Why would she want to be interrogated again?"

Maggie's responding smile was both gentle and mysterious. "Get yourself a cup of tea and join me. Let's chat a minute. What time are you meeting Bethany?"

In the galley kitchen, Dee pulled a cup from the cabinet and selected a tea bag from Maggie's extensive collection of teas. She filled the cup, added the tea bag, popped it in the microwave for a couple of minutes, then leaned over the counter that separated the kitchen from the great room. "Between 12:30 and 1:00. Lunch. Tyler and I are driving into Portsmouth, and he's agreed to let me talk to her alone. She said she's working a twelve-hour shift today and can meet me in the cafeteria."

"So there will be people around."

Dee's eyebrows furrowed. "You think there should be? You think she could be dangerous?"

This time, Maggie was the one who shrugged. "I don't know anything for sure. I know Fletcher doesn't trust her to be completely truthful. Maybe in a public setting she'd be less likely to claim later you said something you didn't. Do you have a recorder?"

Dee shook her head. "But you think I'll need one."

"I do. I'll get my little digital one out of my office before you leave. It's small enough you can slip it in your pocket. Insurance. Interviews can be tricky, and unless there's a record, she can later deny anything you say she told you. I don't know if she's that kind of person, but it's always better to be safe."

The microwave dinged, and Dee removed the tea, tossed the tea bag in the garbage, and added milk and sugar before joining Maggie. In Dee's eyes, Maggie was her complete physical opposite, with her long legs and slender build. The retreat's manager always wore long skirts and practical boots, and her reddish brown curls cascaded down her back. With her feet tucked neatly up beside her, Maggie reminded Dee a great deal of an elegant, quite regal, feline.

As opposed to my resemblance to a fireplug, Dee thought. She tucked one strand of her mostly straight, dark hair behind an ear and tried to avoid sloshing her tea as she sat. "Is David asleep?" she asked.

Maggie nodded and released a long sigh. "I had to take a break. He's been running me ragged this morning."

Dee couldn't help but grin. "You're a great mom. I don't think you can look at him without your eyes being full of love."

Maggie tossed curls back over her shoulder and chuckled. "Shhh. Don't tell him. When he gets older, I'll need him to think I'm serious about time-outs."

"Are you going to homeschool him? It seems like the retreat would be ideal for that, between you and all these writers who have so much information in their brains."

Maggie shook her head. "Fletcher and I discussed it, but I'm not convinced I have the temperament for it. Homeschooling takes a very special kind of mom, and I'm not convinced I'm right for it. The church has a great day care, and we're going to start sending David to a 'mom's day out' in a few months, to get him adjusted to being away from me." She sipped her tea. "Did you homeschool Joshua?"

Dee looked into her cup, her mind drifting. "The last year, Mickey and I planned to do so at least through middle school. Joshua was borderline gifted, and he read way above his grade level. Math and science came so naturally to him that he'd finish assignments before anyone else. His teachers had a hard time keeping him motivated. So he got into a lot of trouble. Fights with the boys who bullied him." Dee knew how sad her smile must look, but these were cherished if painful memories. "We looked into private schooling, but finally just decided to bring him home." She looked up again at Maggie. "On his last tests, he was scoring so high on his reading and math, Mickey and I joked about enrolling him in college."

Maggie watched Dee a moment, then asked softly, "You seem to have let go of Mickey more than you have Joshua."

Dee nodded toward the hallway and the baby's nursery. "You have a son now. You must understand..." She paused to take a sip of tea before going on. "I think if Joshua had been older, if we'd had more time to separate in a natural way...it might have been easier." She shrugged. "You're right, but I'm not sure how to explain it."

"Maybe Tyler has helped?"

Dee looked up sharply. "What?"

Maggie's gentle expression reflected the care in her words. "Dee, everyone can see how close you and Tyler have gotten. How your friendship with him has grown. And he treats you like a princess, even the night...or maybe *especially* the night...he brought you home from the hospital. Do you think you're ready for another relationship?"

Dee just stared at her friend, a wave of uncertainty flooding her. "I don't...I don't know."

Maggie shifted, as if suddenly uncomfortable. "I'm sorry. It's none of my business, really, but Fletcher and I both see how much better you are than when you arrived."

Dee's mind still whirled with a touch of confusion. "And you can't believe how grateful I am to both of you." She looked around the room. "And to Aaron for building this place. I don't know what I would have done without it."

Maggie accepted the change of subject with a sigh and stood up. "Have you seen this morning's paper?" When Dee shook her head, Maggie picked up a paper from the table beside her and handed it to Dee. It was folded open to her column. "That, my friend, is the writing of someone who has a grasp on her world again. Very good."

"Oh." Dee could only manage that small sound as she scanned her own words in print. Slowly her eyebrows went up as her eyes widened. "It's not bad for a midnight scribble, is it?"

Maggie snorted. "It's more than 'not bad,' girlfriend. You need to stop being so hard on yourself. You and Tyler both make me crazy demanding so much of yourselves, as if you weren't—"

"Tyler? So you've noticed it, too?"

"Yeah. He seems to think he's messed this case up. Fletcher thinks he's done fine, given what he's had to work with."

Dee sat straighter, ignoring the drops of tea that splashed out of her cup at her sudden move. "That's what I told him. I fussed at him when we were going to the Bradfords about how hard he was being on himself. I just don't see how he could have done more than he has."

A smile slowly crept over Maggie's face. "Tyler's a good man. One of the best."

Dee paused, suddenly feeling as if she'd walked into some kind of trap, but one she couldn't quite discern. "Yes," she said, suspicion making her drawl out the word into at least three syllables. "He is."

Maggie laughed. "Trust me, I'm not trying to suggest anything. Yet. But I do like how you and Tyler have become friends. You are very cute together."

Heat slid up through Dee's face, and she chewed her bottom lip for a moment. "I like Tyler. I do. I think we're friends. But he's so…Mercer."

Maggie looked puzzled. "What does that mean?"

Dee held up her hand. "Don't get me wrong. That's not a bad thing. But he just seems so…I don't know… *entrenched* here. I mean, after I met him, I fully expected to hear that he'd married his high school sweetheart, who was now head of the local chamber of commerce."

Maggie scowled. "So he's not worldly or sophisticated."

Dee shook her head furiously. "No. That's not…" She stopped, took a deep breath and gathered the words in her head before speaking. "You can't be a cop without having a sense of what the world is about. Tyler isn't provincial or naive. But he loves this place, and I can't imagine him being happy anywhere else. It just seemed to me that he'd be more interested in someone who shared that love of place, like someone who grew up here, or moved here and grew to love it."

Maggie's eyebrows arched. "You don't like Mercer?"

Dee waved her hand in a negative gesture. "I adore it! That's not the point. I won't be staying here forever. You know we all agreed I could stay as long as I needed to be here to recover." She paused looking down at her cup again. "Y'all saved me from my walk on the edge. But I can't live here forever. My family is still in Tennessee."

Maggie watched Dee a few moments, then spoke softly. "Not even if you fell in love here?"

Dee swallowed hard, then stood up. She couldn't

have this conversation right now. "I'm running late. I need to head for Portsmouth." She took her cup to the kitchen, rinsed it, then put it in the dishwasher. When she turned, Maggie stood in the doorway, the digital recorder in one hand.

"Be careful with Bethany Davidson. I'm sure she wants to talk to you because she wants yet another person on her side. The AMA won't listen, the press won't listen. She may tell you about a Jack Bradford you won't like hearing about."

Dee squared her shoulders, ready to return to her work. "Do you know what Jack says about her?"

"Jack says her claims have no foundation. That she has never worked with him in the O.R. and is basing her accusations on hearsay. Her one chance to get her story into the public eye was this case, so she seems a bit frustrated that the press ignored her as a suspect, even though she declares she's innocent."

"Sounds like a mixed-up lady."

Maggie handed her the recorder. "She sounds like a desperate lady. So be careful."

"I will."

"Are you riding in with Tyler?"

Dee palmed the recorder and gave Maggie a quick hug. "Nope. I need to do a bit of girl-type shopping before I meet Bethany, so he's going to meet me after I talk with her. We've got a couple of other people to see, then he'll follow me back."

Dee returned to her room for a notebook and a blazer to go over her light shell and jeans. Slipping the recorder into the blazer pocket, she headed back to her cabin, where her tiny compact car was parked. White and nondescript, the little car had barely been driven since she'd arrived at the retreat. She used it for an occasional run to the grocery store. She'd only driven to Portsmouth once, and as she settled into the seat, she checked her map again for the fastest route. The two-lane Mercer Pike led to the 125, then over to US Route 4, then…. Dee followed the roads with her finger, then dropped the map into the passenger seat and fastened her seatbelt. She could do this.

Turning right out of the retreat, she followed the narrow road into town, slowing a bit when she reached the curve where Tyler had almost hit her. That seemed like an eon ago, even though it had only been a couple of days. Her nose, so tender to the touch, prevented her from sleeping on her stomach—her favorite position— and two tiny bandages still held cuts closed on her cheeks. She checked her face in the visor mirror again, wincing a bit at the bruising that remained around her eye. *At least Bethany's a nurse so I won't scare her to death.*

Dee rolled down the windows and waved at a couple of folks on the sidewalks at Mercer. She did adore this small town and its residents, but she *had* been surprised to find out that Tyler was not married. "Tyler's the heart of Mercer." The wind, swirling strands of hair around her face, absorbed the words.

The words, however, brought to her mind Tyler's face, with his firm jaw and blue eyes that had just enough green in them to make you look twice. And she had looked twice. Dee grinned. More than twice.

Do you think you're ready for another relationship?

Maggie's question hung in the back of her mind. Am I ready? Tyler was certainly on her mind a lot these days, as a close friend, but…she hesitated, even in her thoughts. Anything else, even romantic thoughts of another man, continued to hold a twinge of betrayal for her, as if she were cheating on her husband, who had been dead for three years.

"Maybe. Perhaps not…."

The roar of a revved engine caught her attention, and she checked her rearview mirror, where the grillwork of a large SUV filled the back window.

Dee's eyes widened. "Man, you're too close!" She sped up a bit, but the SUV kept pace, swerving back and forth behind her, doing everything to crowd her but actually bumping her back fender. For more than two miles, the SUV would speed up, closing in on her, then back off a bit. Each time, the grillwork seemed closer, overpowering in her mirror. The SUV darted in and out of the lane, as if seeking to pass, only to retreat in the face of an approaching car.

Dee's heart rate soared as she looked for a place to pull off, but the narrow shoulders of Mercer Pike held no escape, and the steady oncoming traffic left no run for the SUV to pass. Finally, Dee saw the entrance of a subdivision ahead, and she signaled, then slid into the entrance, stopping just inside the dual brick pillars that announced that she was entering Oak Hill Estates. The SUV roared by, and the driver leaned on the horn until the vehicle had passed out of sight.

Dee put a hand on her chest and caught her breath, swallowing hard as the adrenaline eased away. She closed her eyes, pushing away the memory, the mind-crushing memory that just such an incident had started the chain reaction that had led to Mickey and Joshua's deaths.

"Not that," she muttered. "Just one rude driver. Just

rude." Gulping in air, Dee gathered her thoughts and her wits before pulling back out in the road. "Focus, girl. Focus on the case. On finding Carly. On getting through this." Yet, as she focused, it was not Carly's face that settled on her mind.

It was Tyler's.

Tyler hung up the phone, a sense of frustration edging into every muscle. He looked up as Fletcher entered his office and dropped into the chair next to his desk. "That was Rick. They still can't get away, and he's not convinced extra manpower would help at this point."

Fletcher's typically stoic expression remained firm. "But they'll still let us send evidence to their labs for analysis?"

Tyler nodded. "Wayne is taking care of that part. So far, we've had no results on the dress or sandals."

"What about your conversation with Nancy and Jack?"

Sitting forward, Tyler rested his elbows on his desk. "I've been on the phone this morning, tracking down some of his ideas, and I wanted to talk to you about that, even though you are still new to the area. Nancy continues to doubt, but Jack's convinced that this is personal, that it's someone they know. Neither had wanted to consider that for a long time. I think they wanted it to be a stranger."

Fletcher's eyebrows went up. "Of course. No one wants to admit they've been friends with someone who could commit this kind of horror. It makes you feel like an idiot and a fool. But Jack's come around?"

"Yep. He gave me some ideas, including Bethany Davidson again."

"We talked to her. She's angry, but I can't see her for this."

Tyler sat back in his chair again. "Agreed, although after talking with Nancy, Dee decided to talk to Bethany, to see it from a 'woman's point of view.'"

"And you agreed to this?"

Tyler scowled. "Couldn't stop her. Not really. She was pretty determined about it. I'll be right behind her. Nancy also told Dee about a pet store where Carly had made a lot of friends, and a teacher who paid special attention to Carly, even though he wasn't her teacher." He crossed his arms. "A Mr. Riley. Zach Riley. I thought we might have something, so after Dee meets with Bethany, we were going to debrief, then talk to the pet store folks and Riley."

His jaw tightened in frustration. "But when I called the school, they said Riley is on sabbatical and has been since before Carly disappeared. They said they'd try to get me an address, but they think he's on a fishing expedition in Canada."

Fletcher stiffened. "You think he's really out of town?"

Tyler felt his chest tighten. "It's suspicious and the timing is right. But no one is at his house, and his car is gone. Until the school tracks down that address, I can't prove he's not. I gave his name to Rick, and he'll see what he can find out from his end. Wayne is searching our databases here."

"Anybody else on Jack's list?"

Tyler checked his notes. "A Dr. Titlebaum, down in Boston. Apparently, they've feuded over patenting some surgical innovation. Jack wandered off into a lot of technical lingo that I'll have to get in writing if we want to pursue that angle."

Fletcher started to speak, but Peg opened the door and looked pointedly at her son. "Sorry to interrupt, but you have at least two interviews in Portsmouth this afternoon, and you're about to run late."

Tyler stood and reached for his hat. "You're right, of course. Did you print off those directions for me?"

She waved a piece of paper at him, and he took them, speaking to Fletcher as he headed out the door. "I'll keep trying on Riley. There's something there we need to pin down."

"Like why a teacher takes off in the middle of the school year to spend three months fishing?"

Tyler pointed at Fletcher as he headed out the front door of the station. "Exactly! We're getting close. I can feel it!"

TWELVE

With her vibrant red hair pulled back into a neatly controlled pony tail and her scrubs freshly ironed, Bethany Davidson looked as if she had just come on duty, even though she set a tray full of lunch food in front of her as she joined Dee in the hard plastic booth. Dee glanced at the sandwich and fries and idly wondered if all hospital cafeterias smelled faintly of short-order grease and soured milk.

"Hope you don't mind." Bethany popped a fry into her mouth. "This is my longest break in a twelve-hour shift."

Dee shook her head. "Not at all. I appreciate your taking the time to talk to me."

"About the Bradfords, right?"

Dee opened her notebook and set the digital recorder on the table. "I'm just doing a bit of follow-up."

Bethany eyed the recorder momentarily, then went back to the business of cutting her sandwiches in quarters. She then used her knife to neaten the edges. "Are you a cop?"

"A writer."

The nurse paused and put her knife down. "You're writing a book about this?"

Dee shrugged. "Maybe. Right now, I'm just doing a column encouraging people to help if they can." *A book?* The thought hadn't occurred to Dee before, and she tucked the raw seed of an idea away for consideration later.

"Are you going to paint the Bradfords as some kind of saints like all the other reporters?"

"I plan to tell the truth. You don't think they're anything special?"

Bethany took a bite of the sandwich that was so small it didn't even muss her lipstick, and Dee noticed that every single fingernail had the same short clip and smooth curve. Bethany chewed a moment before answering. "He's a surgeon. He's lucky he has any personality at all. Surgeons are notorious for their lack of bedside manner. They tend to prefer their patients unconscious."

"How long have you worked on an operating room team?"

Another fry disappeared. "Almost 20 years with various doctors." She paused, shrugged reluctantly, then took another nibble of the sandwich. "Jack Bradford is normally no better or worse than most. He's good, not great, like some of the reports make him out to be." She spread her fingers and made an arc through the air. "The great Dr. Bradford's tragic loss. The press makes it sound as if the girl were already in the ground." Dee struggled to hide her appalled reaction to the thoughtless statement as Bethany picked up her milk carton, shook it once, then opened it. She slipped a straw through the top and took a sip.

She set the milk down, then fell silent, looking down at her tray, then up at Dee. "I don't like him," she said flatly, "because he let my niece die on the table. He didn't even try to save her. He had no sympathy for us. I have none for him."

Dee felt as if all the air had been sucked from her lungs, and she fought for a breath. Even though Nancy and Maggie both had warned her about the complaint, to hear it so bluntly took her aback. "Are you serious?"

Bethany nodded once, then resumed eating. "That made me a suspect until the cops realized I was in the O.R. almost all day when *his* girl vanished." She waved the knife through the air. "Jack Bradford's beloved child went 'poof,' and they didn't like it that they couldn't pin me for it."

"What happened to your niece?"

"She developed appendicitis on a church retreat at a state park. She was one of the youth leaders, and had led the teens on a strenuous hike. So she just thought the pain was the aftermath of too many wild berries and too much rappelling. She went back to her apartment and took a couple of strong painkillers and went to sleep. By the time her roommate found her, she was comatose. They did emergency surgery, but her appendix had ruptured and the infection had filled her abdominal cavity. They were trying to clean her out when she went into cardiac arrest. The other surgeon wanted to take extreme lifesaving measures, but the great Dr. Bradford just gave up on her. Said the poison was too systemic to save her." Bethany dropped her hands in her lap and stared for a moment at her food. "She died on the table."

Tears blurred Dee's vision and she blinked them away. "I'm sorry. Was she your sister's child?"

Bethany nodded. "But I kept her a lot, so she was almost like my own."

"How did y'all make it through?"

Bethany looked up again and straightened her shoulders with a deep breath. "My sister moved to Colorado to be close to family there, and I joined a grief support group here. And I've requested that I not be assigned to any of Dr. Bradford's surgical teams. Sometimes that's not possible and if I have to work with him, I try to be professional, but to say I have no love for Dr. Bradford is mild."

Dee's eyebrows bunched. "Why didn't you consider a malpractice suit?"

"Have you ever tried to sue a doctor?" When Dee shook her head, Bethany smiled wryly. "For a suit to be successful, you have to get other doctors to agree to the malpractice. That's not going to happen, especially with the great Jack Bradford. My sister and I filed a complaint with the AMA, but medicine in this area is a small community. No one supported us, and whatever investigation the AMA did went nowhere. Even after my sister moved, she was afraid the complaint would be held against me."

"No wonder the police wanted to talk to you."

At that, Bethany actually smiled and reached again for her sandwich. "Actually, I didn't blame them. I certainly had the greatest motive for revenge."

"Why do you think Carly lodged a complaint against you in the E.R.?"

Bethany's eyebrows shot up. "You heard about that?" She paused, then shrugged. "The cops should hire you. I honestly don't know what got into that child's head. I was in Colorado at the time." She nibbled, then swallowed. "But I'm a reasonable woman, Ms. Kelley, not a monster. I'd be the last person to take out revenge on a child. If I wanted to hurt Dr. Bradford, I'd go after him." She sipped her milk. "Instead, when I get the angriest at him, I call my sponsor in the grief group and talk it through." She set her sandwich down without taking a bite. "No matter what the cops think, *that's* how reasonable people cope."

Bethany ate one more fry, then put her napkin over the food. "If Doctor Bradford goes missing, however, I might be responsible."

Dee looked down at her notebook, not wanting to respond.

Bethany made a barely perceptible movement that might have been a shake of her head. "Sorry. Bad joke." She sniffed. "You see, Ms. Kelley, I have nothing to hide in this, and the more I can do to prove that, the more I can prove that Jack Bradford isn't the saint people think he is, and the better off we'll all be." She stood. "Now, if you don't mind, I need to get back to my patients."

Dee stood. "Not at all. Thanks again for speaking with me." She watched Bethany walk away, then sat again, shut off the recorder, and scribbled a few notes about the conversation. As she did, she realized that Bethany Davidson had not been entirely convincing about her innocence. Her details seemed as neat and tidy as the way she ate, and for some reason, that bothered Dee. "As if," she muttered to herself, "she's been spending a little too much time constructing an alibi." Then again, maybe she's just a smart woman who knew the cops would see her as having the best motive.

Dee glanced at her watch, then grinned. Time for lunch with Tyler, then more questions.

As she eased out of the booth, Dee realized she was

actually looking forward to the rest of the afternoon. Digging into her glove compartment, she pulled out the name of a Greek restaurant that Tyler's detective, Wayne Vouros, had given her and Tyler, promising them it was the best Greek food outside his mother's kitchen. She checked the address for Café Nostimo, realized it was only a couple of miles away, an easy find, even for her.

Tyler waited for her, sitting on a bench near the front door, his arms crossed, his expression impatient. "That took longer than we thought."

Dee ignored him, and launched right into her questions as he opened the door for her. "Did you check the alibis of Bethany *and* her sister? Something is just a little too neat there, too convenient."

"We thought so, too. We checked them both for the day Carly disappeared as well as the day Bethany supposedly screamed at Carly in the E.R."

Dee paused, inhaling the welcoming scents of Greek cuisine. "This smells amazing. What do you mean 'supposedly'?"

Tyler headed for the counter to place the order. "What do you want to eat? 'Supposedly' because there was no proof that the encounter happened." He pointed at the menu. "Wayne insists their moussaka is to die for."

"I think I'll stick with a gyro plate. Why would an eight-year-old lie about such a thing?"

Tyler shrugged. "You never made up stuff when you were eight?"

"All the time, but I'm a writer. That's what we do."

Tyler held up a finger, asking her to pause as he placed their order, then led her to a table by the windows. As they settled, he continued. "Carly is a precocious child. Willful and stubborn and very smart. Yet she's still a kid. My guess is that she overheard something, either at home or in the hospital that day, that made her think that Bethany was an 'enemy' of her dad's." He paused, glancing out the window. "Kids don't always understand the subtleties of adult relationships."

Dee nodded, her mind flashing back to Joshua's absolute confusion and fear following one of her fights with Mickey. He didn't understand that parents could fight and stay together. There was so much he never got to learn—

"Where'd you go?"

Dee snapped back to the present. "Oh. Sorry."

"Joshua?"

She sighed. "I just…I just want Carly to be able to grow up. I don't want Jack and Nancy to go through what I have."

Tyler started to respond, but their food arrived, and they waited until the server had left. "They won't. We'll see to that."

He bowed his head for grace, and Dee watched him, a thread of pure admiration and affection for him coursing through her. Fletcher had been right; this man had a passion and drive that ran deep, even as he tried to remain calm and professional. As Fletcher had said, "Too many people mistake calmness for a lack of passion."

Wayne was right about the food, and they lingered over the meal, savoring the last morsels and reviewing her notes from the conversation with Bethany.

Tyler pointed at the notebook as he took another

bite of moussaka. "So basically she didn't tell you anything we didn't already know." He paused, swallowing.

"Apparently not."

He shook his head. "So time to talk to the pet store folks and Zach Riley." He filled her in on what he'd discovered so far about the missing teacher.

"Okay, that's just weird. Why would a teacher leave two months before the end of the school year to fish in Canada?"

He nodded. "Indeed." He stood up. "We're going to have to find out. But first let's see what kind of pet store Carly likes."

They rode together to the pet store, a friendly looking place that faced into the western sun. The rays streamed bright and golden through the windows, and Tyler's face almost glowed in the light as he grinned down at the cat doing figure eights around his ankles. "Patty is going to hate you," he said to him.

"Hope you're not allergic." Dee squatted down and held a hand out to the wiry Siamese. The cat investigated the offering, sniffed, then butted his head against her fingers. She rewarded him with a scratch under the chin, which made him purr.

The young woman next to them, whose name, Gina, was stitched on the royal blue apron she wore over her jeans and oxford cloth shirt, reached down and gathered the Siamese in her arms. "Singer here is the store cat."

Tyler shook his head. "Definitely not allergic, although Patty might be." At Gina's concerned look, he explained. "Patty is my dog. She'll spend a week being annoyed by the cat smell on me." He laughed at the thought of the frantic dog showing her jealousy over this fraternization with another animal. "It'll give her something to do."

Gina stroked Singer between his ears, then set him down, her face turning somber. "We all miss Carly. Her mother would bring her in at least once a week. We groom dogs in the back, and she'd bring Sasha in for her bath. After a few months, we started letting Carly play with the animals in the adoption room. It gave them some exercise and gave her something to do while Sasha finished."

Dee stood, and Tyler watched as her eyes seemed to take in every detail, her gaze flitting from Gina and the cat to the cages and stacks of food and supplies. DeWitt's Pet Friends had the mom-and-pop feel of the pet stores of Tyler's childhood, with its crowded wooden shelves, dark concrete floor, and the very dark and intimate fish room. Inside there, the spotless tanks shone from within, displaying gorgeous fish from around the world. DeWitt's had escaped the coming of the big chain pet stores by maintaining personal relationships with their hometown clients, including many of the doctors at the nearby vet hospitals. The adoption room felt more like a living room than a store, despite the wall of cages filled with lonely-eyed puppies, kittens and the occasional ferret.

"Did Carly make friends with the employees?" Dee asked.

Gina raised her chin and eyed them a bit suspiciously. "Our employees are mostly kids working their way through school. You don't think one of us is involved?"

Tyler met her gaze evenly. "Not directly, but I'd like

to talk to them about their interaction with Carly. Did Nancy ever leave her here alone? Did they ever notice any of the customers paying special attention to her?"

Gina dropped her chin a bit, her defensiveness giving way to her concern about Carly. "Sometimes, her mom would leave her while she ran an errand or two up and down the street. We didn't mind. Carly is a good kid."

Dee let a puppy in one of the cages explore her hand with his tongue. "Did she ever act afraid of anything? Ever say anything to you about what was going on in her life?"

By now, Gina started to relax. "Carly's a bright kid, quite mischievous. Her mother seems to think she's always this sweet girlie child, but Carly could be a whip sometimes. She'd make us laugh talking about school, cutting up and showing off with something she'd read. She once told me she planned to start raising butterflies. One of the teachers at her school was going to help her with that."

Tyler stayed calm. "Did she ever mention anything more about that teacher? A name?"

Gina thought for a moment. "Mr. Riley. Zach Riley." She grinned. "Carly never said much about him, just that he wanted to help her with her butterflies."

"Did you ever see her talk to anyone else, any customer for a long period of time?"

Gina's eyes narrowed. "A couple of times she'd talk to other kids about the animals. She mostly ignored the adults as being too boring." She paused. "Kristy's in the back, she might have seen something. Most of my gang is off today, but I can give you names and phone numbers, if you wish."

"That would be great."

They followed Gina into the back office. His instincts told him this would be another dead end, unless something turned up about Zach Riley. But shortly after Gina introduced them to a bright-eyed teenager, Dee's eyes widened, and Tyler fought to remain calm.

Sure, she knew Mr. Riley, Kristy said. She then expanded on Carly's relationship with her butterfly-enthused teacher with a detail that chilled Tyler to the bone. Four months earlier, Zach Riley had been in the store several times with Carly alone, in the middle of the day, with neither Jack nor Nancy Bradford anywhere in sight.

THIRTEEN

By the time they got back to the café where Dee's car was parked, Tyler had called the school system again about Riley's whereabouts, then tracked down a judge to see about a search warrant for Riley's house. Neither call had favorable results, and the last one left him beating the steering wheel with his palm.

"Judge Compton says the sighting's not enough probable cause for a warrant," he said, in answer to Dee's look of concern. "We don't know for sure if Riley didn't have permission from her parents. He's a good teacher with no complaints against him. No one wants to start a witch hunt."

He hit the steering wheel again and Dee jumped, aware that this side of Tyler's passion caught her off guard, as his frustration sizzled with every word.

"Compton *knows* me! We grew up together. She knows I don't do witch hunts!"

"No, but everyone knows how driven you are to find Carly."

He glanced at her quickly. Then again. He let out a long breath, a bit of his usual calmness returning. "Yes. They do at that." His fingers tightened on the wheel, and he remained lost in his own thoughts until he turned into the café parking lot. As he pulled in next to the little compact, he turned to her.

"You go on back."

Dee's eyebrows shot up. "And what are you going to do?"

He hesitated, then plunged ahead. "Riley lives about 15 minutes out of Mercer—"

"Tyler, don't—"

"I'm just going to look. There's no harm in looking."

"Tyler—"

"Maybe knock on the door."

Dee closed her eyes and shook her head slightly. "I should go with you, keep you out of trouble."

When he didn't respond, she opened her eyes to find that he had leaned a bit closer to her. His entire demeanor had changed and his face had softened. For a few moments, he simply gazed at her, as if trying to read her mind.

When he spoke, his low voice caught her attention. "You want to keep me out of trouble?"

Dee realized she had not truly noticed how rich and dark the blue of his eyes was. "Yes."

"I'm honored." And with that, he kissed her, a slow, sweet brush of his lips on hers that seemed to freeze her in place. As he backed away, he said softly. "Go home, Dixie Dee. I'll meet you at the lodge."

The spell broken, she cleared her throat. "Okay." It was all she could think to say, and she slowly gathered her notebook and opened the door. She got into the little compact, and he waited until she started the engine and pulled away before following her out of the lot.

She still felt a bit stunned as she headed out of Portsmouth, at first glad for the comforting warmth of the car and the brightness of the afternoon sun. Then, as she turned more toward Mercer, the sun increasingly blinded her, and the heat in the car felt stifling. Dee dug a pair of sunglasses out of her glove box and rolled down all the windows.

Much better. The afternoon temperature felt just right for running with the windows down. Indeed, as the wind swirled her brown locks around her head, a sense of exhilarated freedom settled over Dee. The compulsion to find Carly continued to reside in a tight knot in her chest, but for the first time in a long while, Dee's mood soared. She felt good about herself and her writing. Her mind went over her chat with Bethany yet again, wondering about all the "maybes" that remained in the case. *Maybe* Zach Riley was still in the area. *Maybe* Bethany's sister had been in Porstmouth. Then there was the person who had put the dress in Jenna Czock's garbage. Did Jenna know more than she realized? Maybe she saw something… Dee shook her head. Too many maybes. She definitely needed Tyler to help her sort through all the things about this that she did not know.

Tyler. Dee sighed, her mind turning suddenly away from the case as she remembered the gentleness of his hand on her arm, her back, as they'd left the Bradfords. Then the kiss.

That kiss. Unexpected. She knew he liked her but… no one had ever kissed her like that, so soft…so *cherished.*

And it wasn't as if she didn't like being with him. If fact, over the past couple of days, she'd realized how much seeing him every day at lunch meant to her, and

Maggie's questions this morning had sharpened that. Dee enjoyed encouraging him to talk about his own world, and their chats about life in Mercer and his stories about some of its characters had a lot to do with her growing affection for this community. He made her laugh. Seeing him had become an incentive to continuing her exercise program. *When did I start looking forward to seeing him so much?*

Then, as she turned on to Mercer Pike, an image of Mickey and Joshua suddenly flashed before her eyes, and a stab of pain gripped her heart. *I don't mean to betray you. Please.* The thought had an odd desperation to it, and she blinked, tears clouding her vision, made more glistening by the sun. Tyler's face blended with Mickey's in her mind, and she reached to wipe away the tears, remembering the glorious exhilaration of the night before. *I just want to be happy again.* She glanced right, hoping a wayward fast food napkin was left on the passenger seat, and saw a sliver of white tucked in the cushions. She reached for it, tugged the napkin free and dabbed at her right eye.

The first blow to the door of her car came from the left with a sudden, sickening crunch. Dee screamed and grabbed the wheel tighter, barely noticing the black wall of metal in the driver's window. She struggled with the wheel, trying to force the little car back on the road.

She risked a sharp glance to her left, recognizing the vehicle as a large SUV just as it swerved again. The two vehicles collided with a grinding screech of metal on metal. This time the SUV pressed the assault, and Dee fought the wheel, trying to keep the car on the asphalt. The harder she pushed left, however, the more the car slid right with the squeal of tires on pavement. The smell of burning rubber filled the air, and her eyes stung.

Panicking, Dee slammed on the brakes, hoping to pull away from the SUV, too late realizing the mistake. As her car slowed, the front end of the SUV shoved inward toward her front fender, crushing the front end of her car and breaking the tire loose from its housing. Control vanished, and Dee screamed again as the car left the road, her eyes now on the ravine that gaped in front of her.

Dee's head throbbed, and she winced as the EMT dabbed gently at a small cut on her forehead. "What are you using? That stings." She squirmed on her perch just inside the ambulance door. The adrenaline rush from the wreck had left her, but she continued to shake, and she knew her head would hurt for a couple of hours.

The young woman met Dee's gaze briefly, then returned to her duties. "Just something to clean the cut. I'll put an antibiotic on it to cut down on infection. I wish you'd let us take you to the E.R."

Her professional calmness was infectious, but Dee waved away the concern, then stuck her hand under her thigh to hide its trembling. "It's just a cut. I had my seat belt on. I just got jerked around a lot. The headache is from the adrenaline."

"No doubt. And you'll be sore tomorrow. If you think it's anything but a few muscle aches, you go in right away."

Dee nodded, then waited patiently as the EMT finished bandaging the cut, suddenly aware that she could hear a siren in the distance. "Now what?" Dee looked around at the ambulance, police cruiser, tow truck, and three cars from folks who'd stopped to help the tow truck guy get her car out of the ditch. "Don't we have enough folks hanging out?"

The EMT grinned. "One of the guys said Chief Madison was headed this way."

"Uh-oh." She really didn't want to face Tyler after another injury. "Can you hurry up with that?"

"About done." The young woman placed the bandage over the cut and secured it with an extra press of her finger.

"Thanks." Dee hopped down out of the ambulance, but the EMT put a hand on her shoulder.

"Nope. You need to stay put. I don't want you walking around yet. Besides, they're about to bring the car up."

Grudgingly, Dee acquiesced and settled back against the ambulance's bumper. The siren grew ever closer as the tow truck driver set his winch in motion, and the cable dragged the remains of her car out of the ditch.

"Ouch." Dee hadn't really looked at the car after she'd scrambled out of the passenger window and clawed her way up the steep embankment next to the road. So the extent of the damage caught her off guard, and Dee crossed her arms, hugging herself.

She'd bought the little compact after arriving in Mercer as just a way to run around town. It already had almost 200,000 miles on it, and had cost very little. Still, it had been reliable and friendly, and it almost hurt to see the hood caved in and the windshield smashed. Black paint was smeared the length of the driver's side, and the roof looked as if an elephant had recently taken up temporary residence in the middle of it.

When the oversized SUV shoved her off the road, the

car had rolled, coming to rest with the driver's side on the ground. *I wish I had seen the driver, a license plate, anything.* Her mind had been so locked on thoughts of Tyler that she'd been virtually oblivious to the traffic around her.

"Do you need to get your purse out?"

Dee glanced over her shoulder at the EMT. "What?"

The young woman nodded at the crunched car. "Before they put it up on the truck. Do you need to get your purse out?"

Dee shook her head. "I don't carry a purse." She slid her hands into her jeans pockets and took a quick inventory: driver's license, debit card, a twenty-dollar bill, her Swiss army knife in one pocket; her cell phone and retreat keys in the other. Her blazer pocket still held the digital recorder. The car keys were still in the ignition, not that she'd need them anymore.

This is unreal. The tow truck driver tilted the bed of the truck, and as the cable pulled the car up the ramplike bed, every bent piece of metal, every shattered panel of vinyl groaned, creaked and quivered. The driver had started strapping it down when Tyler's cruiser slid into the scene and he shut off the siren. He got out, then stopped when he saw the car.

Tyler put a hand over his mouth and rubbed it back and forth, as if trying to force words back down his throat. He stared at the crushed car a moment, then strode to the supervising officer. They conferred, then, suddenly, the officer turned and pointed at Dee.

Tyler followed his direction, and his gaze locked on her. His brows merged into one thick line as he scowled, and his eyes darkened to an intensity that made her sit a bit straighter. As he stalked toward her, her stomach tightened in a way that was part fear and part anticipation—she really wanted to avoid the coming confrontation, yet she truly felt relieved to see him.

The EMT glanced once at Tyler and backed a discreet distance away.

Tyler stopped in front of Dee, towering over her perch on the ambulance bumper. All the muscles in his jaws seemed chiseled into place as he examined every inch of her face. When his stare shifted abruptly to the EMT, the young woman snapped to attention.

"She's okay. Abrasions on her elbow and knee from her climb out of the ditch, that cut on her forehead. No signs of concussion. She refused transport."

Tyler's cop stare snapped back to Dee, and she almost flinched when he spoke, his voice a low growl. "You need to go to the E.R."

She shook her head, ignoring the slight throbbing at the back of her skull. "I'm all right. Promise."

"Tell me what happened."

Dee told him, leaving out the part about tears and thoughts of him. Maybe later.

Tyler looked again at the car, then back at her. "Was it intentional?"

The question caught her off guard, and she frowned, thinking. "Surely not. I'm sure they were just distracted..." Her words trailed off as she remembered the fierceness of the second hit. *Second hit?*

"What?"

She let out a long breath. "They hit me twice. The second time, they kept pushing."

He nodded, and his shoulders dropped a bit as he reached out, one hand cupping her cheek. "What am I going to do with you?"

The gentle touch, the soft question left Dee speechless. Her mouth opened as if to respond, but no words emerged as she watched his face slip from "cop mode" into tenderness, then back again as he dropped his hand from her face and stepped back.

"Stay here. I want to talk to the guys. I'll drive you home. I'll take care of you."

Dee watched him walk away and slowly closed her mouth. Her cheek still felt warm from his touch, and she covered the spot with her own palm.

"Well, it's about time."

She turned to the EMT behind her. "What?"

The young woman grinned. "Every single female in Mercer has been waiting for this to happen. For the unshakeable Tyler Madison to fall in love."

Dee looked over her shoulder at Tyler. "In love?" The warmth in her cheek seemed to spread through her chest as she thought about the kiss. "You really think he's in love?"

The EMT finished stowing her medical supplies in the ambulance. "Looks like it to me. You're about to dash the hopes of a lot of girls in town."

Dee shook her head, turning back toward the scene as she watched Tyler talk to one officer, then another. "I don't think…he can't…"

The EMT paused to check her bandage again. "Tyler never did exactly what people expected him to. So, yeah, he can." She stepped back. "I'm going to finish the paperwork. I'll keep an eye on you, and yell if you get dizzier or need to lie down." She picked up a clipboard and moved away.

A strange weakness settled over Dee, but she knew in her bones it wasn't from the accident. Her mind flashed back over a dozen conversations at Laurie's café, the soft warmth of Tyler's hand whenever he touched her, the strength of his arms and chest when he'd carried her from the car into the lodge house that night after the attack. His whispered, "Ride easy, Dixie Dee."

Then there was that kiss.

Their first meeting at the café had been almost accidental. He had come in to get to-go coffees for his first shift officers because their coffeepot was on the fritz. She'd been unable to sleep the night before and had showed up early for breakfast. They'd met a few days before at the retreat, and he'd greeted her warmly, starting a story about the café that he finished over breakfast, the coffees momentarily forgotten.

An accidental breakfast, but the lunches had become so regular that she felt spurred on during her morning walks. She relished his company, and felt drawn to be with him. But love?

He stopped the tow truck driver for a moment's chat, then moved to one of the men who'd witnessed the wreck, pushing his hat back a bit on his head and leaned toward the shorter man. She had always appreciated Tyler's classically handsome face, the square jaw and close-cropped blond hair, although that look had never been her type. Her type was Mickey, thin, lean and dark, with...

Suddenly the scene of another accident flooded her memories. She'd been driving, like now, and she'd survived that one, too.

Mickey and Joshua had not.

Dee closed her eyes and tried to force back tears. *Oh, Tyler. I just can't. Not yet.*

She opened her eyes again, and found Tyler, his eyes dark and worried, watching her closely.

The sounds of rage from upstairs plastered Carly to the bed. She hugged the pillow to her chest and curled into a tight ball, pushing herself as close as possible to the headboard and the wall beneath the window.

This was bad. The worst Carly had heard. Her captor's fury appeared endless, and each eerie scream would escalate into words Carly couldn't understand, shouts that unleashed a frenzied wrath on the world, and would culminate in a hard thud that sounded as if furniture would any moment crash through the ceiling and into Carly's tiny world.

She had so hoped for a good day, a nice day. When her captor had come into the room earlier that morning, Carly had expected to be scolded for not finishing the packing. Instead, the breakfast tray had been delivered with only one statement expressing the captor's disappointment: "Anything not packed by tonight will be left behind."

Left alone, Carly had packed the books and a few toys, along with the more interesting DVDs. She had left out her book about the girl detective, Robin Kane, and enough art supplies to spend the afternoon drawing, sheet after sheet covered in sunshine-lit days and beautiful butterflies. She had almost enjoyed those final hours, and had not packed those remaining pieces until just before bedtime, even keeping a couple of crayons and one piece out for later.

But the good day had been spoiled by this raging fit, which had started the minute the captor had returned home. Carly had left her paper on the desk, shoved the crayons in her pocket, and retreated to her bed.

Finally…silence. Carly remained quiet, waiting for the next thump or scream, but none came. Instead, the air filled with a long, keening wail, like that of a badly wounded animal. The sound echoed through the house, and Carly felt the hair on her arms prickle. Gradually, it faded, leaving the house bathed in silent darkness.

The tightness in Carly's muscles eased, and she released her pillow and slipped beneath the covers. Turning her face toward the ceiling, she prayed, her voice a bare whisper. "Lord, I'm going to need a lot of help. Soon. I know You're listening. It's getting worse. Scary worse. Help."

FOURTEEN

Tyler picked up his pace, his running shoes making a hypnotic padding rhythm on the pavement beneath his feet. Beside him, Patty ran with an even gait, her panting providing a syncopated counterpoint to the sound of his shoes. He hadn't planned to run tonight, but he needed to burn, to try to force out of his mind the image of Dee's crumpled and ruined car. The very thought of it knotted his muscles again, and Tyler ran harder, Patty now lagging behind on the leash.

Tyler headed to the park, wiping sweat from his brow as he turned a corner. He didn't even slow to offer a "hello" to the folks in the neighborhood whom he usually stopped to chat with. Tonight, he couldn't linger. He desperately needed to push himself physically, to exhaust his mind and body, to try to forget the images of that afternoon. The images of the little compact sitting atop the tow truck's bed, of Dee at the back of the ambulance, continued to hover in his brain, locking a sheen of ice and fear around his heart.

As a cop, he'd seen hundreds of wrecks. He had witnessed a few happen right in front of him. He'd investigated his share of them. He had seen people walk away unhurt from destroyed vehicles, and he'd known of people who died in cars that looked relatively untouched. Yet none of them had come close to dropping him to the ground as if someone had jerked his feet from beneath him. He'd frozen when he first saw the car because he'd been terrified to hear what the supervising officer had to say about the driver.

That she had survived virtually untouched had been a miracle, and Tyler once again murmured a feverish prayer of gratitude. What's more, she'd gotten out of the car and clawed her way up the bank without help. This was definitely not the wounded bird that Fletcher and Maggie had spirited to New Hampshire from a dark bedroom in Tennessee. This was a woman prepared to fight for herself.

And when he'd spotted Dee at the back of the ambulance, clearly all right, the breath had returned to his lungs in such a gust that he'd almost choked. All he wanted to do in that moment was gather her in his arms and keep her safe and beg her not to get any more involved with this. He longed to take her home, cradle her close and keep her safe the rest of her days.

But she's not mine to do that.

Instead, he'd returned home and reached for his running shoes.

A tug on the leash made him look down and back. Patty, whose energy sometimes seemed endless, looked up at him with pleading eyes. He slowed for a few moments, then stopped under a tree. Patty dropped down on the ground and rolled in the grass, then stretched out on her side, ready to rest. Tyler sat next to her, bracing his back against the tree. He scratched her belly, prompting her to twist onto her back to give him better access, her tail thumping wildly on the ground. He grinned. "You're shameless." She wiggled in response, then rolled back to her side.

Tyler drew his knees up and rested his arms across them, looking around the park. The tree sat atop a small rise, not far from a cluster of tree-shaded benches that was his usual retreat here. He preferred this section of the park because he could look down the slope into the heart of Mercer, then to the rolling hills beyond. Now those hills were a dappled carpet of various shades of springtime green, but he'd also sat here many times in autumn, surveying the bright colors that quilted the land in the fall. "Why would anyone ever want to leave this?"

Patty responded with a low woof, then sat up, watching him.

"She's no longer the wounded bird," he told the dog. Patty tipped her head to one side, curious about the words, his odd tone of voice. Tyler stroked her back but looked to the hills again. *Would Dee leave when she healed, got fully back on her feet and restarted her writing career? That was why she was here, after all. To heal. To recover. To leave.*

The thought chilled him.

Why? Why was Dee different from the other women he'd dated? There had been quite a few women in his life since his first kiss at sixteen. A couple even had almost been serious, at least in the eyes of the world. But the thought of them leaving had never soaked him in the dread that this did. Over the past few months, Tyler had come to realize that he didn't just *enjoy* seeing her—he *needed* to see her. He didn't just want to have lunch with her every day. He wanted to have lunch with her forever.

"Patty, I've got it bad." He scratched her under the

chin, and she nuzzled his hand. "I hope you like her."
He grinned. "I hope she likes you."

He turned his gaze upward, focusing on the dashes
of the waning sunlight and dimming blue sky he could
see through the dense canopy of leaves over his head.
"Lord, is this what it feels like to meet your soulmate?
To want to be with her all the time? To think you'd go
crazy if she left?"

The whispers of the spring leaves swirled around him
as thoughts of Mercer and Dee blended in his head. They
went nowhere, but they did calm him. A good thing. With
a sigh he patted the peekapoo at his side. "Let's go home."

Back at his house, Tyler added cool water to Patty's
dish, and he left her lapping thirstily as he headed
upstairs for a shower. Calmer, he found himself making
plans. He wanted to take Dee out, have a real date.
Maybe he'd take her to Portsmouth or Manchester to a
fancy restaurant, show her that he could treat her like
a princess as well as a friend.

Padding to his computer, his bathrobe soaking up the
last of the dampness left on his skin from the shower,
he intended to look at a few restaurants. Instead, he
found an e-mail from Dee waiting for him.

Hi, Tyler,
I've attached my notes on my conversation with
Bethany Davidson. I know it doesn't reveal anything
you didn't already know, but I promised to send
them. You were so silent on the ride back I didn't
think you wanted to talk about it then.

You got that right. He had been so flushed with anger
and fear that he had not been able to speak on the short

ride from the wreck site to the retreat. He just hoped he hadn't scared her.

In light of that promise, I also wanted to tell you that I'm going to talk to Jenna Czock tomorrow afternoon about her finding the dress. Do you want to come along?

Are you kidding? I'm not letting you out of my sight again.

By the way, do you know if Bethany's sister also has red hair?

Good question. As he'd realized today, Tyler found Dee's instinct about people and details to be insightful. For instance, Bethany's alibis had struck him as "convenient" from the beginning, but they'd never been able to break them. She had been in the O.R. when Carly vanished, and she had a plane ticket to prove the trip to Colorado. Maybe the sister was the link.

I promised Maggie I'd help her with a few things around the retreat tomorrow morning, after I sleep late enough to rid myself of this adrenaline headache. After Maggie's chores, I want to work on my writing for a bit. I have an idea for the next column, and an article I want to pitch to a parenting magazine that's published me before. Also, I've started a blog. So I want to go to Jenna just before she closes the shop.

But…you'd better call me if you find Zach Riley! Don't you dare go off to see him without me. :)

I'll also have to deal with the wreck, I guess, the insurance and all that. Sorry you had to see me all bedraggled this afternoon. Sorry you were upset with me.

I missed you at supper, and will *really* miss you at lunch tomorrow. Hope you can make it to supper tomorrow. I think we need to talk.
Always,
Dee

Tyler leaned back in his chair, his gut tightening a bit, this time with a touch of anticipation. "Does she see it, too?"

OK, so maybe not a fancy restaurant. He smiled at the pretentiousness of the thought. Dee wasn't much for "fancy." They did need to talk, but where? What better place than the retreat? Or maybe even better…. He grinned as he hit the Reply button, typing quickly.

He had just sent his response to Dee when a thumping made him look down. Patty sat at his feet, a stuffed toy in her mouth. He scowled teasingly at her. "I thought I wore you out on our run." She pranced backward, waiting. Time to play.

Tyler stood, his resolve once again giving him a sense of peace. It would work out. *It would.*

"You can't just tell him you don't want to see him anymore!" Maggie sprayed furniture polish on another cloth and tossed it to Dee. "You're involved with Carly's case now!" Maggie's tone became even more frustrated. "Besides, I know you like him. My word, girlfriend, every time you look at him you light up like the proverbial Christmas tree!"

Dee turned to dust a set of shelves on the far wall of

the great room so that Maggie couldn't see the heat that stung her cheeks. "I do like him. I like being with him more than you can imagine. But when I'm with him, I feel as if I'm betraying Mickey. I didn't start out that way, but that feeling gets stronger every time I'm around Tyler."

"That's because you're falling in love with him."

Dee clutched the cloth in both hands and rested her forehead against one of the shelves. "I just don't think I can do this."

Maggie paused, then went to Dee and tugged on her arm. "Come here." When Dee resisted, she tugged harder. "Come sit with me a moment."

Relenting, Dee followed Maggie to the sofa in front of the silent and dark fireplace. As they sat, Maggie pulled the cloth away and took both Dee's hands in hers. "Answer me something: When you married Mickey, how many men had you dated?" Dee hesitated, and Maggie shook her hands. "How many?"

"Two."

"Either of them serious?"

Dee shook her head.

"So Mickey was the only man you'd ever been with, the only one you ever loved. For most of your adult life, you've never thought of being with anyone else. And there's always going to be a place for him in your heart. You don't stop loving them just because they die."

Maggie's own eyes moistened, and she reached up to brush away a tear. "But you also can't close your heart off because he's gone. What you feel is normal, but so is moving on with your life. That's why you're here, remember? I know you didn't intend to fall for Tyler. I certainly know that neither of us expected it. Heavens, Fletcher once told me he thought Tyler would always be a bachelor because he was too set in his ways. But you two clicked. That's rare. It's special. Please don't give up on that."

Dee eyes stung with tears, but none fell. "I just intended to get on with my career."

"I know. But you shouldn't overlook opportunities right in front of you either." Maggie straightened. "Now, didn't Tyler offer to take you to Jenna's shop?"

A grin spread slowly over Dee's face. "Actually, his e-mail said he wanted to talk first, then we'd go to the shop. He didn't *ask* so much as he *told* me he'd pick me up about three."

Maggie stood. "Yep, that's Tyler. He's nothing if not direct." She checked her watch as a sleepy wail sounded from down the hall. "You have about fifteen minutes to put some lipstick on. I need to get David a snack." She stepped away from the couch, then paused. "Promise me you'll give him a chance."

Dee hesitated, then nodded, and watched Maggie head down the hall toward her son. She stood herself and headed down the other wing to her room. "Lipstick," she muttered, entering her bathroom and staring into the mirror. "As if any makeup would help this face." With the tip of her finger, she lightly traced each small cut, the fading bruise around her eye. "I look like I ran through a barbed wire fence." Dee sighed and backed away. Then she paused, stared at herself a bit longer, then reached for the light bronze tube of lipstick on the sink.

Tyler's cruiser pulled up in front of the retreat lodge promptly at three. When Dee stepped out, Tyler took off his hat and held the car door open for her. She settled in and he joined her. As he pulled out of the long driveway, he cleared his throat. "So what did you want to talk about?"

She hesitated, then shook her head. "Nothing important. It can wait. Have you heard anything new on Zach Riley?"

Tyler's brow furrowed and his mouth tightened, as if that wasn't what he expected her to say. "No, and yes. Nothing new on Carly, and I did speak to the school again. I talked to the secretary, who insists Riley is in Canada, says she got a postcard from him."

"Hmm. Like work colleagues never lie for each other."

He shrugged. "I told her if I didn't have a call from him by this afternoon, I was going to call the RCMP and have *them* find him."

She faced him. "You're going to sic the Mounties on him?"

"I'm tired of being evaded by someone who's increasingly becoming a person of interest in this. While we wait to talk to Mr. Riley directly, Wayne is talking to his neighbors, more of the folks he worked with." He paused. "Which I didn't get a chance to do yesterday."

Dee looked down at her hands. "Sorry."

"I'm just glad Mom alerted me as well as the regular patrol." He took a deep breath. "Wayne's also researching the names of black SUV owners in this and the surrounding counties."

"That'll take a while. It's a popular car around here. One tailgated me when I was headed to Portsmouth. I had to pull over to let him get by."

He glanced at her, alarm growing in his eyes. "Did you tell the officer this yesterday?"

Dee looked at him, confused. "Why should I?" Then

her stomach tightened as recognition hit. "You don't think it was the same driver, do you? They would have had to follow me all the way to Portsmouth and back. Why not just hit me then?"

Tyler's hand tightened on the steering wheel until his knuckles whitened. "Where did you pull off?"

Dee thought back to the double brick pillars with their elegant bronze plaques. "Oak Hill Estates."

He nodded. "That's not far from the 101. Too much traffic from there to Portsmouth. Too many potential witnesses. They may have just waited until you returned."

Dee pushed back in her seat, annoyed and a little worried. Her sense of security had started to return since she'd been staying in the new room at the retreat, and she'd almost decided to resume walking into town.

"I guess it wouldn't have been a good idea to walk to Jenna's this afternoon."

Tyler made a noise that sounded as if he'd swallowed a goldfish, and he glanced at her, his eyes narrow with worry. "No."

His reaction almost pushed Dee to giggle, which she knew he wouldn't find amusing. "You wouldn't worry, would you?"

Tyler turned up Fifth Street, skirting the walking mall of the Fourth Street arts district and Jenna's floral shop, and brought the cruiser to a halt in front of the park's bandstand. To the left of the bandstand, his favorite cluster of park benches sat in the shelter of some of Mercer's oldest trees, towering oaks that cast a wide, dense shade, even in mid-spring.

"Do you mind if we sit here for a few minutes before we go to Jenna's?"

Dee looked out over the quiet, sunny park and almost sighed. "It looks peaceful."

"And we haven't had a lot of peace lately." He got out, then walked around to open her door. Dee got out, and as he shut the door, she took his arm, realizing it felt like the most natural thing in the world to do.

Give him a chance. Maggie's words echoed in her head, and Dee fought the urge to sigh. She would try. And the warmth and strength of his arm under her hand did feel…comforting.

Tyler curled his own fingers over hers, and she glanced up at him. "You forgot your hat."

He looked down at her, startled. "What?"

She pointed at his head with her free hand. "You always wear your hat when you get out of the car."

His mouth jerked in amusement, as if he were enjoying a private joke. "I don't think I'll need it here."

They both fell silent as they walked to the bench with the best view of the park. As they settled, Dee looked around at the luscious scenery, raising her chin a bit as the wind brushed her hair away from her face. The town lay before them like a Norman Rockwell painting, small, historic and perfectly American. The mill pond at one end of Main Street glistened in the afternoon sun, like a pool of liquefied gold. The granite city hall at the other end anchored the town with a solid, unmoving permanence. The hills beyond reminded her in many ways of the hills of Tennessee. They were part of the same mountain chain, so she shouldn't be surprised that the rise and fall of them felt familiar, almost like home. *He must love this place. It's probably where he comes to relax.*

"So…do you come here often?"

It was out of her mouth before she could stop it, the

oldest pickup line on the planet, heard in bars all over the world. Tyler's eyebrows shot up and his eyes gleamed with humor. "I beg your pardon?"

Heat scalded her cheeks. "No. I mean…I didn't mean it like…" *Shut up, Dee!* She clamped a hand over her mouth. "Oh."

Tyler Madison threw back his head and laughed. The sound burst from him like the suddenness of a refreshing spring shower. At first, the heat in her cheeks increased and tears of embarrassment stung her eyes, but then she gradually began to giggle, relaxing as his laughter slowly subsided. Tyler wiped his eyes, then turned to her, gripping her hand in both of his.

"You have always been able to make me laugh."

"Because I'm an idiot when I'm around you?"

He shook his head. "Anything but." He let out a long breath. "Look, Dee, I don't know what's happening between us, but since you've been involved in this case, you've made me crazy."

A pinprick of disappointment stung Dee, and she knew it showed on her face. "But I thought I was helping."

Tyler's eyes widened. "You are! No, that's not what I meant." He stopped, looked down, then took a deep breath before looking at her again. "You didn't join this case by choice. You were thrust into it the minute you found those sandals. But every move has put you in some kind of danger. I can't get away from that. It distracts me. I can't focus on Carly because I worry about you so much. And that's not like me. I've been obsessed with finding Carly since the day she disappeared. I just don't know—" He broke off and looked away into the distance. "I'm not saying this very well."

She squeezed his hand. "I think you're doing just fine. My turn." He met her eyes, and she faltered a bit, but went on. "This afternoon, I told Maggie that I was going to suggest we not see each other for a while."

His eyes took on a slightly panicked look as his face paled. "Now, wait—"

She held up her hand to stop him. "I changed my mind. But don't you see, we're thinking along the same lines." She fought to keep a touch of desperation out of her voice. "Whatever is happening between us, Tyler, has been building just the way *we* needed it to. Slowly, over time. Neither one of us makes a move quickly, and there's some part of me that still feels as if I'm betraying Mickey when I'm with you."

"Dee—"

She plunged on. "This case shoved us together. It made you worry about me, and made me realize I had to get past that feeling. I thought some time apart might help." She paused, shaking her head. "But I can't walk away from Carly any more than you can. We have to get a grip on *us* so we can find *her.*" She shook her head slowly, looking down at their clasped hands. "Mickey will always have a place in my heart. He was the first man I ever truly loved. But I have to move on and find a way to love again. To love another man."

His smile was gentle, with a loving sweetness to it. "Any chance I could be that other man?"

Dee's eyes burned as she reached up and touched his cheek. "I think you already are."

Tyler leaned closer, tilted his head to one side and kissed her, a bare whisper of a kiss, a soft kiss of hope, of promise. As he drew back, Dee closed her eyes, her voice hushed. "Do that again."

He did, releasing her hand and taking her into his arms, holding her close long after the kiss ended. Dee slid her arms around him, leaning her head against his shoulder, taking in the rich scent of his cologne and relishing the reassuring comfort of his strength.

After a few moments, Tyler whispered. "It's getting late, if we're still going to talk to Jenna."

With a deep sigh, Dee pushed away from him. "True. It shouldn't take long. And I need to get back to the retreat by six for dinner."

Tyler stood, pulling her up. "*We* need to get back to the retreat by six."

She nudged him playfully. "You just want a free meal."

"Well…the company's not bad, either."

Dee laughed, and let him help her into the car. He drove back into downtown and parked near the station, and started the short walk toward Fourth Street. They hadn't gone far when Wayne shouted from the doorway of the station. "Tyler!"

They turned, and Wayne pointed at Tyler. "Phone call! Urgent!"

Tyler checked his watch, then looked up at Dee. "Let me get this. Jenna doesn't close until five."

"Okay."

He held the door of the station for her, and she settled on one of the visitor chairs, ready to make small talk with Peg. There was barely time for hello, however, before Tyler barreled out of his office and grabbed her by the arm.

Trotting beside him, she almost hit the door as he yanked it open. "What's going on?"

His face darkened like a sudden storm. "Zach Riley is back in town."

Tyler covered the ten miles to Zach Riley's secluded nineteenth-century cottage in record time. Dee clutched the door handle the entire time, refusing to show any fear at the tight turns as he took along the rural New Hampshire lanes.

As the cruiser swung into Zach's gravel drive, however, Dee suddenly grasped Tyler's sense of urgency. In front of the house sat a small truck, half loaded with cardboard boxes. Zach Riley was leaving town—again.

"Fishing in Canada? Hardly." Zach Riley poured coffee for both of them and handed over two sturdy ceramic mugs. The bespectacled teacher motioned at the sofa in his living room, which was one of the few clear surfaces in his house. "Please, sit."

Dee perched warily on the edge of the cushions, her gaze taking in as much detail as she could in the room smothered in books, display cases filled with butterflies and stacks of papers. On one stack of magazines, a cat snoozed, his chest rising and falling in a soft rhythm.

Tyler joined Dee, addressing his questions to the teacher. "Why would the school tell us that?"

Zach shrugged and eased down into an ancient wing-back chair. "I'm not sure. I didn't tell them where I had gone, mostly because it wasn't their concern. The secretary, who is a good lady, by the way, probably just assumed it."

Tyler's voice didn't relinquish its driving tone. "So where did you go?"

The teacher sipped his coffee, then set the cup on the floor near the cat. The feline, smelling the aroma, stirred and stretched. "Let's say I had a crisis of conscience." Zach adjusted the collar of his flannel shirt.

"Over the past couple of years, I've grown increasingly dismayed with my ability to reach the kids." He gestured to the stacks of books. "I'm too studious. Not exciting enough." He sat straighter in the chair. "Carly was actually the last child who seemed to respond to me." He paused, shaking his head. "I only heard about her disappearance a couple of weeks ago."

Dee felt incredulous. "A couple of weeks? How could you not—"

Tyler cleared his throat and shifted uncomfortably on the sofa. "So where did you go?"

"A hermitage. Totally cut off from the rest of the world."

Tyler sat quite still. "To pray?"

Zach nodded, and Dee stared at both of them in surprise. "Pray about what?"

At Zach's feet, the cat began lapping coffee from the cup. Zach glanced down but did not move. "I applied to a seminary in Texas. They accepted me. That's why I'm packing."

"So how did you feel when you heard about Carly?" Dee asked. "Since she's your favorite student."

Tyler stiffened, but Zach didn't seem ruffled at all by the question. "Devastated. I couldn't think. That's actually why I decided to come home. I found out the seminary accepted me after I got here. Things are in a bit of an upheaval, or I would have already come to see you."

Zach stood and walked to a bookshelf, sifting through several notebooks. He finally pulled one free, ripped a sheet off the top and handed it to Tyler.

"I made a list. I wasn't Carly's teacher, but I was around her a lot, especially after she found out that I was something of an expert on butterflies. She's obsessed with them."

Dee's eyes widened. "She sought *you* out?"

Zach finally smiled, a small, sad one that didn't quite light up his eyes. "Yes. Carly can be quite driven when she sets her mind to something. I fully expect to see her in public office someday. She's relentless."

He pointed at the paper. "We'd use field trips to check out pet stores and museums. That's a list of people who showed a little too much interest in Carly for my comfort. She's a beautiful little girl. That sometimes drew in folks that made my skin crawl."

Tyler glanced over the list of names. "Anyone make her nervous?"

Zach shook his head. "Carly never met a stranger. She'd talk to anyone about butterflies or God."

Dee stood up. "God?"

"When I told Carly I would be gone in a few weeks, she told me that God would let me know what I needed to do. Unshakable, that one."

Dee stepped closer, enough that Zach stiffened, obviously a little uncomfortable with her closeness. "How tall are you, Mr. Riley?"

Zach looked down at her. "Six-four. Why?"

Dee turned to Tyler, waiting. He got the message and stood with a wry smile. He reached to shake Zach's hand. "Don't mind my assistant here," he said, with a nod at Dee. "She's a little obsessed herself."

"Oh!" Zach stepped over a stack of books. "One more thing." Carefully, as if he were handling precious china, he pulled a wooden case from another shelf. Turning, he handed the case to Tyler.

"This is a display of my rarest finds. Would you see that Carly gets it when you find her?"

Tyler glanced down at the rows of stiff and beautiful butterflies. "I will."

They left, picking their way cautiously through Zach's belongings. In the car, Tyler glanced sideways at her. "That was a little obvious, don't you think?"

She shrugged, then grinned at him. "You'd already excluded him. Didn't hurt to verify that he was too tall." Her smile faded. "He wasn't the one who attacked me."

Tyler backed the cruiser out of the drive. "No. In fact, I'm surprised the man even kills the butterflies he collects."

"But I bet he'll make a good preacher."

When they arrived back at the station, Tyler turned to Dee before getting out. "Let me get Wayne started on these names, and I'll put the case in my office. It won't take long."

Dee glanced at her watch. "Look, Jenna's about to close. This shouldn't take more than five minutes. There's no real need for you to come. I'll come back to the station when I'm finished and fill you in."

He lowered his chin and looked at her, eyes narrow. "Be careful."

She grinned, raised up on her tiptoes and kissed his cheek. "Don't worry."

"Hmph." But he relented, opening the back door of the cruiser to get the case as Dee headed up the street, walking past the art gallery on the corner and into Jenna's floral shop.

A bell dinged lightly as she entered, and she inhaled, taking in the blended, almost overpowering scent of hundreds of flowers. The aroma of roses was the most prominent, although Dee could also detect the heady odors of lilies and chysanthemums.

Jenna emerged from the back, wiping her hands on a cloth, which she folded and tucked into the pocket of the apron covering her slacks and knit shirt. Her face lit up with a bright smile. "Dee! I was expecting you earlier."

Dee sighed. "I know. I'm sorry I'm late. Something came up at the last minue."

Jenna nodded. "I understand, but now I'm in a rush. I was just about the close up. Then I have a couple of deliveries to make. Would you mind riding along with me?"

Dee hesitated. She didn't really want to leave, especially with Tyler waiting on her.

Jenna responded immediately to her hesitation. "We could stop by my house if our chat runs longer. It's on the way to the retreat. I would be glad to take you home afterward. I've not seen Maggie in a while. It would be nice to say hello." Without waiting for more hesitation, Jenna pointed behind her. "Let me lock up the back, and we'll go out the front."

Five minutes later, Dee sat on the passenger side of Jenna's late-model sedan, a vase of roses held between her knees. As they passed the Mercer Police Department, Dee pulled her cell phone out of her pocket and thumbed in a text message to Tyler.

She smiled to herself. *So he won't worry.*

FIFTEEN

Jenna turned her car into the gravel drive, bumping the tires up over a raised curb designed to keep the rainwater from the street out of the drive. The car rocked a bit on its shocks as she braked in front of one side of the two-car garage. She tossed her head, causing her long black hair to shift and flow over one shoulder, and smiled at Dee. "We'll go in the front."

Dee tucked her notebook under her arm and got out, following Jenna to the door. "I appreciate your taking the time to talk to me."

Jenna shifted the keys in her hand and selected the one for the front door. "Not at all. I've wished I could be more help since I found that little girl's dress. I don't know what I can tell you, but we'll find out."

They entered a comfortably appointed but tidy living room and dining room combo, darkened by thick drapes. Jenna snapped on a lamp near the sofa. "I keep the drapes closed to help with the bills." She paused to set her purse and keys on the table beneath the lamp, then took a deep breath. "Look, do you mind if I take a quick shower? I feel like I'm coated in junk from the shop."

"Not at all. I can just sit in here and get my questions ready."

Jenna's smile widened, then she pointed to a swinging door at the back of the dining room. "Thanks. There's soft drinks in the fridge. Oh, and bottled water, if you'd prefer." She turned toward the hall, then stopped, looking thoughtful. "You know, I may have seen the guy at my garbage clearer than I told Tyler. I've really been thinking about it. We'll talk more in a minute." With a perky lift to her step, she left the room.

That's good news. If Jenna's description matched her own recollections of the attacker in the woods... Feeling a bit smug, Dee headed through the swinging door into the kitchen and found an avocado-colored refrigerator. She opened the fridge and stood there, a bit surprised at the ample supply of cans filling the shelves. *Wow, she must really love the caffeine.* Dee pulled out a soda and let the door swing shut. She popped the top, allowing the fizz to settle a moment while she looked around the kitchen.

Like the rest of the house, the kitchen was clean and tidy, but dated. She had grown up with the wallpaper, and the table and chairs against one wall showed their age through the simple wear-and-tear of use. The entire house had a musty odor, like a house that had been shut tight for many years. It felt odd, but Dee tried to shake it off. *Maybe florists just don't make enough money to redecorate just because trends change.* Still...the house gave her the creeps, and she hoped Jenna would return soon so she could get out.

That's when she saw the artwork on the fridge, a child's drawing of a curly-haired dog and little girl, a kite soaring over their heads. Oversized butterflies in a kaleidoscope of colors danced around their heads. Dee frowned, puzzled. The drawing looked new, but in the car, Jenna had mentioned that her daughter, Elaine, had been living with her father in Oregon. And the style looked familiar, making her think she'd seen this drawing before. Her eyes narrowed as she focused on the artwork, trying to remember. *Butter-flies, I've seen these butterflies.* Her breath stopped as a flicker of recognition hit her memory. The Brad-fords'. She'd seen them at— *No. Oh, no.* A frisson of anxiety slid down her spine, and she shivered. *No, it couldn't be. No.*

She pushed the thought away, and stepped back from the fridge. *No. Wishful thinking. Probably a neighbor's child. It can't be Carly.*

Without thinking, she said it aloud. "Carly? Carly!"

The result was a frenzy of tapping from beneath her feet that made Dee yelp and jump away from a vent in the floor. She looked down, eyes searching frantically. In her confusion, Dee called aloud, "Who's tapping? Carly!"

"Yes!" The scream was young and frantic, echoing through the floor vent. "I'm Carly Bradford."

The words dropped Dee to her knees. "Carly! Where are you!"

"Basement! Help me! PLEASE!"

Dee scrambled on hands and knees toward the vent, every muscle shaking with adrenaline. She put her mouth close. "How do I get there?"

"There are stairs. I don't know where they are."

Tyler! She had to get Tyler. "I'm going to call the police. Hang on!"

Dee grabbed one of the chairs to pull herself up,

clawing at her pocket for her cell. She flipped it open and dialed 911.

"No, I don't think so." The voice behind Dee was adamant and commanding.

Dee spun to face Jenna, just in time to see an aluminum bat in its downward swing. She threw up her arms, but they were not enough protection. The bat found its mark and Dee's world slammed into darkness.

Tyler stared at the text message from Dee, both confused and irritated.

He hated text messages. Half the time he had no idea what they meant. Even his mom was better at them, to the point that it had become an in-house joke among the other officers.

Fletcher opened his office door, and he turned the phone toward him. "Do you have any idea what this…" His words faded as he looked at Fletcher's troubled expression. "What's wrong?"

The older detective held his own cell phone in one hand. "That was Maggie. She wanted to know if you are still bringing Dee back in time for dinner. Dee apparently sent her a text message, but, Maggie's not sure if it meant you were going to bring her home or if she planned to walk back. Didn't you say you two were going to talk to Jenna Czock at her shop?"

Tyler nodded, standing. "Dee wanted to ask about the person Jenna saw at her garbage. I brought in evidence from Zach Riley and she went without me. She didn't expect it to take more than a few minutes, then she sent this." He handed Fletcher his phone as he checked his watch, the old fear returning to the pit of his stomach. Where *is* she? "Did Maggie try her cell?"

Fletcher glanced at Tyler's phone again. "Maggie's tried to call it four times already. No answer. If I'm reading this right, she left with Jenna to deliver some flowers, then planned to meet you at Jackson's Retreat at six." He paused. "Flowers?"

Tyler tried to ignore the tightening knot in his stomach. "Jenna usually closes at five. It's after six. I can't believe I lost…maybe they went to Jenna's house to chat."

"Maybe." Fletcher wasn't convinced. He handed back Tyler's cell. "I'm going to see if Wayne's finished that list of SUV owners in the area."

As Fletcher turned, Peg pushed by him, her face pale, her breath coming in short pants.

"Mom, what's wrong?"

She swallowed hard. "We just got a 9-1-1 call from Dee's cell, but it went dead before we could get anything else."

Tyler grabbed his hat. "Fletcher!"

The gentle rocking of the SUV woke Dee by sending waves of lightning-hot pain through her head and left arm. She groaned, a sound almost drowned out by the soft sobs coming from the backseat and the sounds of a 1970s rock band booming out of the speakers. In the front seat, Jenna hummed along with the music, occasionally singing an off-tune word or phrase.

Dee opened her eyes, squinting against the light, and tried to get a bearing on her surroundings. Clearly, she was in the back compartment of the SUV, her hands tied behind her back, exacerbating the pain in her arm. Her left biceps had taken the brunt of the blow from the aluminum bat, and Dee hope it hadn't cracked the bone.

A tight, dry feeling at the edge of her hairline told her the bat had reopened the cut from the accident and that the blood had matted in her hair.

A large cooler blocked her view of the back hatch, and several matching suitcases pressed her body up against the back of the seat and covered her legs. Dee sighed. It would be impossible to get to one of the back light panels or raise up enough to get the attention of a passing car. Besides, with the dark tint covering the windows and the height of the SUV, a tall man would have to be standing next to the car, peering directly into the windows, to see anything unusual. Dee couldn't imagine Jenna letting anyone get that close.

Tyler had been right when he suggested the kidnapper planned to move Carly. Jenna must have been preparing this move since before the sandals went missing. But why had she taken Carly in the first place? "And why didn't she kill me there in the kitchen?" Dee's throat felt raw, irritated by the question, and she swallowed hard.

In the backseat, the quiet sobs suddenly fell silent, and there was a distinctive sniff. Then another.

Dee froze. She hadn't thought she had spoken loud enough for anyone to hear her. But…maybe…

"Carly?"

Sniff.

An odd wave of emotion, a braid of both fear and hope, flooded Dee, and she took a deep breath. "Carly, if you can hear me, don't say anything. If you can, prop your arm up on the backseat."

A rustle of cloth against vinyl answered her, and Dee twisted so that she could look up. There, above her head and resting gracefully on the back of the seat, a small delicate hand wiggled fingers at her. In the front, Jenna still hummed along with the '70s band.

Dee cleared her throat. "Excellent. My name is Dee. Sit tight, baby. There has to be a way out of this. Keep an eye on the highway signs, okay? We'll need to know where we are."

The fingers wiggled again, then the small hand dropped out of sight.

Dee took another deep breath. *Have to think. What can we do? What have we got?* She took inventory. Her cell phone was missing, probably still in Jenna's kitchen. There might be something she could use as a weapon in the luggage. Hair spray, maybe. *Can't get to that with my hands tied. Need to break or untie—*

No. It hit her abruptly. Not untie. Cut. Her pocket knife was in her left pocket. *But how…*

The SUV hit a bump, and the pain in Dee's left arm sharpened. She bit her lip to try to control the pain, then shifted, trying to ease the bend in her arm. The movement only resulted in her banging her head against the cooler, and she squeezed her eyes shut, trying to stop the throbbing.

The cooler.

Her eyes snapped open, and she stared at the large white box, now understanding the substantial number of drinks in Jenna's fridge. Dee smiled slowly, a germ of a plan forming in her head. Had to work out the logistics…and she wondered how long it would before Jenna had to stop for gas.

Tyler peered through the window of the garage as Fletcher knocked one more time on Jenna's front door.

Although her car still sat in the driveway, the garage space in front of it overflowed with the accumulation of normal household goods and yard tools gathered over twenty years in the same house. The other side of the garage, however, had clearly been used to house a vehicle. The open space, free of any clutter, also featured oil spots on the concrete floor.

He straightened and called to Fletcher on the porch. "Think we have probable cause to go in?"

"No. We have no clue where that call came from and we have no proof that Dee is still with Jenna. She could have tried to walk home and fallen along the way." Fletcher stepped off the porch and back out into the yard, looking over every feature of the house.

"You're thinking like a defense lawyer." He slammed his fist into the garage door. "I should never have let her go talk to Jenna alone."

Fletcher's mouth twisted. "Look, I know you're falling in love with Dee, but you can't keep her wrapped in cotton the rest of her life. As she's recovered, Maggie and I have discovered a distinctive willfulness in the girl."

Heat blossomed in Tyler's face and he peered again into the garage window. "I thought I was being discreet. Is it really that obvious?"

Fletcher snorted. "You look at her the way I look at Maggie. What do you think?"

Tyler looked at his friend a moment, his mood growing more somber and fearful by the minute. *Where was she!* "I just wish she saw it the way you do."

"What makes you think she doesn't?"

Tyler looked around the yard, then off into the distance, trying to ignore the hard tug in his heart.

"Over the past few months, seeing her almost every day…." His voice trailed off.

"I think the feeling is mutual. She can't take her eyes off you. She may not be ready for a relationship yet, but your foot is definitely in that door."

The thought of Dee watching him made Tyler redden again, and he cleared his throat and motioned toward the house again. "I want into this house. Think it would do any good to check the backyard again?"

Fletcher shook his head. "No. I don't. If Jenna *is* involved, I doubt she'd leave any other clues for us. The dress did its job. If she's not, there's nothing to find anyway. And I'm not completely convinced she *is* involved."

"Why not?"

Fletcher glanced toward the house again. "There's no clear motive or connection to the Bradfords. And she's a mom. She told me she thought all little girls deserved a chance to grow up like her Elaine."

An icy wave of dread washed over Tyler and he froze, staring at Fletcher. "She said what? When?"

"When we were in the house that day, I heard some tapping in the basement, and she said the pipes had air in them. The dishwasher was running, which she said made the pipes pop. She said she had to find a good plumber because Elaine had come home. She took me upstairs, showed me Elaine's room, some of her drawings, how proud she was that she'd returned from being with her father out west."

"Oh, dear God," Tyler muttered, his fear forcing the prayer out of him. "Lord, what has she done?"

His mind flashed back through all the stories his mother had ever told about the one great unsolved mystery of Mercer. In the late 1970s, Jenna Czock's daughter Elaine had been killed while camping with her father. The town had rallied around Jenna and her husband Todd. In the long run, Jenna had seemed to handle it better than Todd, who never quite recovered. They divorced within a few years, and Todd moved to the Pacific Northwest. Portland. Jenna opened the flower shop and went on with life. If Jenna thought Elaine had returned....

"What's wrong?" Fletcher's mood turned instantly alert and guarded.

Tyler moved toward the front door at a run. "Now we have probable cause."

Fletcher followed. "What are you talking about?"

Tyler tested the front door, then took two steps back. "We no longer need a search warrant. You just gave me probable cause."

"Tyler—"

"You're still new around here or you would have known." His voice, low and gravelly, dropped almost an octave. "Elaine Czock died when she was eight. If she thinks Elaine just returned from out west, there's a good chance she's either hallucinating or—"

Drastic alarm crossed Fletcher face. "—or she has an eight-year-old in the house."

"Back me up."

Fletcher reacted immediately to stand behind Tyler, gun drawn, ready to cover as Mercer's determined police chief thudded open the front door with one sharp kick.

SIXTEEN

For the next half hour, the only sound in the SUV came from Jenna, whose out-of-tune humming grated on Dee's nerves even as it reassured her that Jenna suspected nothing. The world had grown dark as they drove, and Dee knew from the patterns of the streetlights that they had left any city behind. From the frequent stops and turns, followed by only short periods of straight driving, Dee guessed that Jenna's route didn't involve interstates or toll roads, and the occasional groupings of lights reminded her of Mercer. Back roads and small towns. *She's playing it safe.*

Finally came the turn Dee had been waiting for. Bright lights settled steadily over the SUV and Jenna braked. As she shut off the engine, Jenna spoke firmly to Carly. "I have to get gas. Look over the seat. Is she still unconscious?"

Carly's head popped up over the seat, and Dee smiled at her, then winked.

Carly dropped back down. "She's not moving."

"Don't try anything. Stay in your seat. If you try to run or signal anyone, I'll kill her. I mean it. Understand?"

"Yes."

Fear turned to rage in Dee's gut. *Why would she do that to a child?*

"I'll be right back." The car door opened, then slammed.

Dee cleared her throat. "Carly, can you hear me?"

The young voice sounded defeated. "Yes."

"Where is she?"

"She went in to pay."

Cash, not a card at the pump, Dee thought. *No record, but it gives us a little time.* Dee took a deep breath and gathered her courage. "Then listen to me carefully. First, she's not going to kill me or she would have already. Don't let her threaten you like that. Okay?

"Okay."

"Now, listen. Stay in your seat. If she sees you get up, she'll realize I'm awake. Where are we?"

"The last sign said Willimantic."

"What state is that?"

"Connecticut."

"Okay. When we get back on the road, ask her if you can get a drink out of the cooler. Don't do it while we're stopped so she won't get it for you. When you reach over the seat, open the cooler, but then reach into my jeans pocket. There's a knife there. Pull it out and put it in my hands, then get your drink. Do you think you can do that? You'll have to move quickly."

A brief silence followed, then Carly spoke, her voice much stronger. "If Nancy Drew and Robin Kane can do it, so can I."

Dee almost laughed with fearful relief. "That's my girl."

"I prayed for you, you know."

Dee grew still. She couldn't have heard right. "What did you say?"

The voice on the other side of the seat was even stronger. "I asked God to send me a rescuer. One of His warriors. You may not be one of His warrior angels, but you're still a warrior. He sent you to answer my prayer. I just know it."

Dee remained silent. How do you tell a child that God doesn't always answer prayers? *God doesn't answer...*

If You do answer prayers, send Tyler. Please. Tears flooded Dee's eyes and soaked the mat beneath her head.

"This house looks like something from the 1970s." Tyler stared at the furniture and the heavy drapes. "A 1970s cave."

"In New York, it's called retro and is quite trendy in some areas."

Tyler glanced at Fletcher, but his friend's face showed no amusement. Both men had burst into the living room in a crouch, guns drawn, listening for a response to their thunderous entrance. When none came, they had slowly prowled the house, looking for signs of Dee, Carly, or Jenna. The hallway and bedrooms were clear, although both had stared in disgust at the bedroom decorated as if Elaine still lived there. Now they headed back to the kitchen. Tyler reached it first and stopped dead in the doorway, a chill radiating throughout his body. "We'll need Wayne."

"What do you see?"

He stepped aside and pointed to the floor and the door of the fridge, where a spray of red droplets revealed the violence that had taken place here. Dee's cell phone lay in the middle of the floor, smashed.

Fletcher muttered something under his breath, then put his hand on Tyler's shoulder. "There's not enough blood for a serious injury. Don't jump to any conclusions yet. Where would she have kept Carly?"

Tyler stared at the phone. "She tried to call for help. She tried to call me."

Fletcher squeezed his shoulder. "Carly."

Tyler forced himself to look away from the blood, dread turning his mind numb. "Probably the basement. All these old houses have one."

The second door they tried opened onto a set of narrow stairs leading down, and Fletcher flipped the light switch on the wall with his elbow. A pale yellow light cast harsh shadows down the steps. At the bottom, however, another switch turned on a series of bright fluorescents, revealing the basement as a pristine work and storage area. The room smelled earthy but not damp, and a dehumidifier hummed pleasantly in a far corner. Shelves lined the walls, most filled with neatly labeled plastic storage containers. The uniformity of the shelves was broken only by an upright freezer, and a set of stone steps leading up to a slanted set of wooden double doors that Tyler knew opened onto the backyard. In the middle of the floor a worktable held bins containing pots, silk flowers and the tools for arranging them. Tyler walked to the table and peered into the bins. They were as tidy as the rest of the basement. "Lovely. Crazy and a neat freak."

"Which means she left in a hurry or she would have cleaned the kitchen." Fletcher spoke but did not look at Tyler. Instead, he stared at a section of shelves near the staircase, his head tilted to the left.

Tyler joined him. "What do you see?"

Fletcher holstered his gun, then pointed. "See how that set of shelves is out of sync? Each shelf is about three inches higher than the ones to either side. That would drive a true neat freak crazy."

Looking down, Tyler saw the reason. "They're on casters. Now I wonder why she needs this set to roll." He holstered his own weapon, grabbed one side of the section and pulled.

The padlock on the old, wooden door behind the shelves dangled open from a latch, more evidence of a hasty departure. Tyler opened the door slowly and flipped on the light. The two men stared at the little girl's room, from the bookcase to the dresser, and the crumpled bed. An open trunk stood in one corner, toys and clothes spilling out of it.

"I'm going to call Rick." Tyler heard the fierceness in his own voice. "I think that Amber alert should go out now."

The SUV pulled back into traffic, and Jenna resumed her humming. Just before they left, she'd pulled Carly from the backseat and escorted her to the bathroom. When they returned, Carly tossed a piece of toilet paper over the back of the seat. As it settled, Dee shifted to see four words scribbled in crayon: "I left a note."

Dee felt her heart leap. Everyone she'd talked to about Carly had sounded as if the child had spent life as a spoiled, fragile princess. Apparently they had been overlooking both her resourcefulness and creativity.

Dee braced her feet against the side panel of the SUV and pushed, trying to make her pocket and hands more accessible. After the rough bumps of a railroad and two more turns, the road smoothed out, and the sound of the tires settled into a steady drone. Jenna stopped humming, but turned the music up a bit.

"Can I get a drink out of the cooler?"

The sudden request startled Jenna, who let out a "What?" that sounded almost like a yelp.

Carly repeated the question, adding a "Please, ma'am" on the end.

Jenna hesitated. "Can't you wait? We're almost there."

"I'm really thirsty."

Another hesitation. "Okay, but be quick about it."

Carly bounced up, leaning precariously over the backseat. Just as Dee has instructed, she opened the cooler and pretended to look inside as her hand reached down. Dee felt the small fingers slip into her pocket and close around the knife. Another swift movement, and Carly pressed the knife into her palm. She pulled a soda out of the cooler, dropped the lid shut and settled back into her seat.

"Fasten your seat belt," Jenna called, and Dee heard Carly click the belt shut. "Is she still unconscious?"

"She didn't move." Carly sounded confident and comfortable.

Don't get cocky, Dee thought. *Stay scared.*

The knife, still warm from being in her pocket, felt like an old friend. Being careful not to drop it, she turned it slowly in her hands until one finger found the tiny slot in the main blade, just right for her fingernail. Grasping it firmly in one hand, she tugged on the blade, but it wouldn't budge. Frustrated, she changed her grip slightly and tried again. She'd used the knife hundreds of times, but never while her hands were tied behind her back.

This time, the blade opened smoothly, but nicked the side of one finger. Dee bit her lip, and kept turning the knife until she felt it press against the bonds. Sawing steadily, she felt the plastic cord give, then snap away.

Elation shot through her as she brought her hands around in front, rubbing them furiously as the blood rushed into her fingers, causing them to sting and burn. Then she held herself still for a moment. The sudden sense of freedom made her want to crawl over the seats and wrap her hands around Jenna's neck, but she knew that would only put them all at risk.

Instead, Dee cut the cords binding her feet, then reached for the nearest piece of luggage and unzipped it slowly, quietly, beginning a methodical search through the contents.

Willimantic? How in the world did she get that far south already? Tyler's mind had been filled with a numbing buzz since the Amber alert had turned up a sighting in Connecticut. His eyes focused solely on the white lines in the road, his thoughts on nothing but getting there. Finding her. Finding *them.*

But something in the back of his mind tickled a memory. Something about Willimantic. He frowned. *Why is that familiar?*

Fletcher snapped his cell phone shut. "Rick again. Said the Amber alert went out all over New England, but there's no other sightings. Wayne confirmed that Jenna owns a black SUV and called Rick with the VIN and license. The Connecticut troopers are swarming the area."

Tyler turned onto the interstate, switching on his headlights to push back the descending dusk and the blue lights on the cruiser to part the traffic in front of them. His foot pressed harder on the accelerator, and the cruiser, which they'd taken from Wayne once he'd arrived at Jenna's, responded smoothly, like a big cat ready for the chase.

As if reading Tyler's thoughts, Fletcher continued. "They must have left sooner than we thought. The customer who found the note at the gas station gets Amber alerts on her cell, and had already seen it. When she saw the note from Carly, she called 911 as well. The Connecticut troopers are on the lookout for the SUV and New York has been notified."

"Anything else?"

Fletcher referred to the notebook in his lap, where he'd been taking notes. "Not yet."

Tyler's hands tightened on the steering wheel, trying to keep his focus on the road in front of him. In his mind, however, the image that hovered was Dee, injured, terrified. He increased his speed, even as he prayed. *Lord, keep them safe. Don't let my mistakes become their fate.*

Jenna hadn't been kidding about how close they were to their destination. Dee had given up on the search of the luggage, finding nothing but clothes and a few books. She'd returned the knife to her pocket.

Yet only about ten minutes had passed before the SUV slowed again and turned onto a rocky road that caused it to buck and jolt. Jenna proceeded slowly for five minutes or so, then stopped again and shifted into park. "I'm going to open the garage door. Stay here."

She got out and closed the door.

Dee fought the temptation to look. "Where are we?"

"Looks like a farmhouse," Carly whispered. "Shhh."

Jenna got back in, let the SUV roll about twenty feet, then shut it off. A few minutes went by as Dee heard Jenna shifting around in the front seat, as if she were looking for something. After a satisfied, "There you are," Jenna got out, came to the back, and lifted the hatch. Dee blinked in the sudden light, then realized Jenna held a revolver in her right hand.

Jenna grinned. "Yep, I somehow knew you'd wiggle free. Quite the clever girl, aren't you?" Her grin vanished. "Get out."

Dee swallowed hard, and struggled to climb over the luggage and out of the SUV. She stood, but her muscles quaked from being confined in the same position for so long. "Why did you bring me with you?"

Jenna looked a bit puzzled. "Because you know. And I want you to tell me."

It was Dee's turned to be confused. "I know what?"

"You know why all these people keep trying to take Elaine from me."

Dee's eyes widened, and she glanced quickly at Carly, who stared at them from the backseat. "Elaine?"

Jenna's lips pursed. "Of course, Elaine. Who else?"

"I thought you said Elaine lived with her father."

"Oh, I just told a few people that so they wouldn't think I was crazy." She waved the gun around blithely, making Dee wince. "Oh, she went off with her father all right, but when he came back without her, most of the town thought she was dead. But I knew Todd—" She stopped, her mood darkening suddenly. "Todd!" Her voice rose to an angry scream. "Todd had taken her! He took her from me! But I knew. I knew!"

The abrupt storm vanished as quickly as it appeared,

and Jenna took a calming breath. "I knew she'd come back. She'd find her way home." She turned a loving look on Carly. "And there she was that day in the woods. I'd searched those woods for her so often, almost every day, then just like that, she was there."

The storm returned. "Of course, he'd turned her against me! I tried to make her remember, but, of course…" She stopped, and steadied the gun again, aiming at Dee's chest. "Enough for now. Elaine needs supper." She used the gun to point toward a door at the front of the garage.

Dee walked slowly, getting her bearings as she moved as Jenna directed. The SUV sat on one side of an oversize garage; the other spot held a white sedan from the early '90s. Around them were an assortment of tools, yard equipment, paint and oil cans, and building supplies. Many of the tools had a fine layer of rust on them, and a sheet of drywall propped against one wall had a spray of mold growing up one end of it. Everything about the garage smelled old—rancid oil, thick dust, dried grass, and musty paper.

"Where are we?"

"My parents' house." Jenna stopped and opened the back door of the SUV and motioned for Carly to get out. The girl scrambled out and fled to Dee's side. Dee put an arm around her as Jenna motioned for them to continue walking.

"Why are we at your parents' house?"

"I thought if Elaine could spend some time with her grandparents, it would help. And we need a place to spend the night before heading south."

They stood to one side as Jenna unlocked the door and ushered them into the farmhouse kitchen, switching on a light near the door. The house smelled even mustier than the garage, and each step they took stirred up small whorls of dust.

"Mama!" Jenna called. When no one answered, she motioned at them with the barrel of the gun. "Stay here. If you run, I'll shoot."

"We will." Dee kept her voice calm and reassuring. "We'll be here."

Jenna went through a swinging door into a dining room. "Mama! Daddy! Where are you?"

Dee turned, examining the clearly abandoned kitchen. Spider webs draped from the window to the curtains, and everything was unplugged—the toaster, the coffeepot, the microwave. Even the refrigerator, which stood open.

"Dee?" Carly's barely audible voice made Dee look down into the pale, terrified young face. "Is she crazy?"

Dee dropped to her knees and wrapped Carly in what she hoped was a reassuring hug. "She is. But we'll get out of this. I know we will."

Carly buried her face in Dee's shoulder and clung to her. "I know we will, too. I asked God to help us, and I know He won't let us down."

Dee closed her eyes and tightened the hug. "Let's hope you're right."

SEVENTEEN

"Well, can they at least pinpoint the area?" Fletcher once again had his phone pressed to his ear, as he scribbled in his notebook. After a moment, he closed it, then grabbed the door handle as Tyler swung through another turn, still heading south toward Willimantic.

"What's going on?" Tyler's hands ached from his fierce grip on the wheel.

"There was another sighting from the Amber alert, but all they had was the name of a road."

"Where they still in the Willimantic area?"

Fletcher looked down at the notebook. "Yes. Heading south on Highway 289. Rick's pulling all public records on Jenna, trying to see if she has a connection to the area."

In the back of Tyler's mind, that nagging something finally clicked. "She does. Her parents lived there."

Fletcher stared at him. "What? How do you know that? Would her parents really help her on something like this?"

"They won't. They died last year. There's a faster way to find their address than public records. Call the office and ask Mom to pull her Christmas card list from two years ago. It's on the computer. It'll be quicker."

Fletcher stared at him. "You're joking."

"Nope. Jenna's parents spent a lot of time in Mercer, and put everything they could into the search for Elaine after she disappeared on that camping trip with Todd. They were on Mom's Christmas card list every year until they died. Complications from diabetes took him after a long illness, and she went with a heart attack a few weeks later. Both were in assisted living, and the house was transferred to one of Jenna's aunts. It'll take a while for Rick to ferret that out. Believe me, the list is faster."

Fletcher flipped open his phone and dialed again, stating his request to Peg. He listened for a few moments, then wrote down an address, and repeated it to Tyler. "Lebanon, Connecticut."

"That's about ten or fifteen minutes out of Willimantic. Call Rick." A faint wave of hope made Tyler smile. "See? There are some advantages to living in a small town."

"They must be visiting my aunt. They don't usually go out of town without telling me, but she doesn't live far. They'll be back by morning. I'm sure of it."

Carly pressed herself a little tighter against Dee's side. They had settled in the living room, and Carly and Dee perched on the edge of a mohair sofa that gave off a new whiff of dust every time they moved. Jenna sat in a sturdy, cane-bottom rocker across from them, her toes making a rhythmic tip, tip, tip, each time she rocked forward. The pistol lay on her lap, one hand covering it protectively.

The outside lights under the eaves of the house blazed brightly, casting harsh circles of white light in the front yard. Inside, Jenna had turned on only a small lamp with a thick Tiffany-style shade, creating a small golden glow tinged with green near the sofa. Her rocker sat mostly in shadow. She faced the front door and plate glass window next to it, and occasionally, she'd scan the yard.

"I can't believe they need groceries, but that's okay. We have sandwiches in the cooler. That'll do until we leave in the morning."

"Where are we going?" Dee glanced from the gun to Jenna's partially shaded face.

Jenna's smile held no warmth, and her eyes continued to have a distant, unfocused gaze. Her voice took on an uneven, sardonic tone. "Well, you aren't going anywhere. Mama has a root cellar, and you'll stay there until we are long out of reach. Elaine and I are going south. We have relatives in Kentucky. In the mountains. They'll keep us safe, and out of reach from anyone here. They won't be swayed by Jack Bradford's power. Big man doctor."

Jenna yanked the gun out of her lap and pointed at Dee, her eyes suddenly wild. "Why does he want my daughter! I saw your article! You wrote about it! You know! Tell me!"

Carly and Dee jerked back, and Carly let out a short squeal. Dee grabbed Carly with one arm, and held the other hand out in front of them, a sudden surge of anger racing through her. "Jenna, stop it!" she yelled. "You're terrifying Elaine, and I can't tell you if I'm dead!"

Jenna froze, then slowly lowered the revolver, an exasperated gasp leeching from her. "I know. I know! I just…" Tears streamed down her face. "I just don't want to lose her again! And no one will tell me why. Why they want to take her from me."

"I know," Dee said, her voice flat. "I lost my son three years ago. No one could tell me why then, either."

Jenna quieted. "I had heard that when you first came to town. How?"

"A car accident. I watched him die. And I wanted to die, too."

Jenna's dark hair quivered, and her fingers trembled on the gun. "They didn't find Elaine. Todd said she fell into the river. But they didn't find her." Her hand reached out toward Carly. "Because she's still alive. She's not dead after all. She'd been in town all along. Todd, he just wanted to keep her from me. She's here."

Tears clouded Jenna's eyes as she stroked Carly's hair. The child flinched and pressed closer to Dee, but did not back away.

Dee squeezed Carly tighter and struggled to keep her words even, her voice calm. "How long ago did Elaine go off with her father?"

Jenna's eyes narrowed, and the harsh shadows in the room aged her beyond her fifty-something years. "April 12, 1979." She took a deep breath, and her eyes lost their focus again. "I'll never forget that date. A lifetime ago."

"Is Todd still in Portland?"

After a pause, Jenna nodded.

"Did he marry again?"

Another nod. "Sweet girl. I spoke to her once on the phone. They had three children. But he used to call me every May 4th." She smiled. "Elaine's birthday. He never forgot."

"How old are his children now?"

She shrugged. "In their late twenties, I guess. They are younger than Elaine was…is…was…" Her voice trailed off, and she looked at Carly and swallowed hard.

The tears resumed silently, flowing in steady rivulets down her cheeks and dripping onto her blouse. "Elaine is thirty-eight."

Jenna took a deep breath and seemed to come into the present, and her gaze moved from Carly to the window behind them. Then she motioned for them to stand. "Get up. Your friends are here."

The cruiser slid to a halt on thick grass slick with dew, and both men sprang out, crouching behind their open doors. Behind them, a phalanx of Connecticut state troopers and the dark sedans of the FBI followed, lining up across the yard, their headlights creating a stark field of intense light and black shadow.

Tyler growled with frustration and fear as he looked through the plate glass at the front of the house, spotting Jenna in the rocker, waving the gun wildly at Dee and Carly, who were sitting on a sofa that sat at an angle from the window. Fletcher stood briefly, blocking his body from the house with the cruiser, and motioned for everyone to keep back.

Lord, I can't lose her. I can't. Help us. Tyler took a deep breath. *Help me. What do I do?*

As he watched, Dee stood and spun around, staring out the window, her eyes wide with terror, her gaze searching the yard frantically. She needed him.

Then, deep, deep in his soul, Tyler Madison knew what he had to do. It felt right, so right that a sense of relief washed over him. *Is this from You?* he prayed. *Lead me.* With that, his sense of resolve strengthened.

"I'm going inside." He stepped from behind the car door.

Fletcher's barked response shot through the night. "No! Tyler! Wait for the negotiators!"

Tyler shook his head, reached for his hat. He placed it on the hood of the cruiser, then unbuckled his gun belt, lifting it free from his body. "Fletcher, I've known Jenna Czock all my life. She'll let me approach."

He walked slowly, his hands held wide, toward the front door of the house, never taking his eyes off Jenna.

Through the window, Jenna stared at him, comprehension washing over her face. They watched each other a few more moments, then an insane darkness fell over Jenna Czock's eyes.

"What are you doing?" Dee's horror-filled whisper caused Carly to whimper at her side as they stared out the window. An army of cars had flooded down the driveway of the farmhouse, pulling out into the yard, their headlights surrounding the house like a siege machine of law enforcement. In the middle, Tyler Madison stood, his arms held well away from his body.

Fear for Tyler surged through Dee, and too late she realized the mistake she'd made by turning her back on Jenna. Jenna's left arm circled her throat, pulling her backward and closing off her airway. Dee clawed at the choking arm until she felt the barrel of the revolver against her cheek.

"Stand still!"

Dee stopped struggling, but managed to choke out, "Let me breathe!"

Jenna's hold on her loosened slightly, and Dee gasped in a lungful of air, all too aware that Jenna's height gave her the advantage in this contest.

Carly backed away from them and toward the door,

her eyes wide, and her face even paler than usual. She focused on Dee, tears brimming in the corner of her eyes. "What do I do?" she begged.

Silence hovered in the living room a moment, then Dee spoke softly, her voice still raspy. "Let her go, Jenna. Let Elaine go."

"No. Never. Not again! She's here with me now. She has to stay!" Her arm tightened on Dee's neck again, the gun pressed harder against her face.

Panic seared through Dee, and she tried to push it back, knowing she would never sway Jenna if she couldn't control it. *Lord, help us. Help me.* The prayer was a desperate cry, the kind God had never answered for her before. *Please.* She twisted her head, looking at Tyler.

Watching her, he turned his hands palms down, closed his eyes, and mouthed one world. *Calm.*

A prayer. Tyler was praying, too.

Whatever happens, Lord. Keep them safe. Please. Keep Tyler and Carly safe. Don't take them from me again.

Again. The thought brought a quietness to Dee, a sureness that she would not go through such a loss again. Carly was not her child; Tyler not her husband. But...

"Listen to me," she whispered. When Jenna did not respond, Dee continued, suddenly grateful for a conversation she had with Maggie earlier that day. "We both lost the dearest person in the world to us. Our child. There's always going to be a place for Elaine in your heart. You don't stop loving her just because she's gone."

Jenna's arm tightened on her neck, but Dee pressed

on. "You told me. April 12, 1979. Jenna, I believe with all my heart you are not crazy. You just still hurt. Unstoppable pain. But Elaine would be *thirty*-eight, not eight." Dee struggled for breath. "Don't make another mother go through this. Don't make another mother hurt this bad. Let Elaine go."

More silence, then Jenna responded in a voice choked with grief and tears, as she eased her grip on Dee's neck. "She's not Elaine."

"I know. Let *her* go, too."

As if she understood both requests, Jenna nodded. "Open the front door slowly, child. So they can see you."

Carly obeyed, cracking the door only a little at first, then wider. Shouts echoed all over the yard when the officers realized who was standing in the doorway. In the glare of the lights, Dee saw Tyler move forward, approaching the house with a slow, determined gait. When he was close, he motioned for Carly to come out.

"Go on, child." Jenna's voice now held the affection of the grandmother she might have been if Elaine had lived. "They will take care of you."

With one backward glance at Dee, Carly opened the storm door and fled down the steps and into Tyler's arms. He squatted, pulling her close and stroking her hair, whispering to her. The sight of Tyler with this little girl caused a fist to tighten around Dee's heart, and an almost unbearable love for the man flowed through her, a deluge of the sweetest kind.

And he had come. For her. For Carly. He'd found them.

"This isn't going to end well, you know." Jenna's voice, so tender when she'd released Carly, had hardened again.

"It can," Dee whispered desperately. "We can walk out. I'll tell them everything." She winced as the barrel pressed harder into her cheek.

"No. You were right. I know what I've done. I have to let her go. Let it all go. You were right. The pain never ends. It has to end."

"Jenna, we can—"

"Shut up. Here he comes. Your hero."

Dee watched as Tyler handed Carly over to a female officer, then he approached the house again, slowly, with Fletcher lingering behind him. Reaching the porch, he opened the storm door and stepped inside, his hands still held wide, his voice low, even, and comforting.

"Jenna? You know me. Let's talk."

Jenna stepped back, pulling Dee tighter against her. "I don't think so, Tyler. We all know I've been through too much." Her voice caught, but she cleared it and continued. "Done too much. Hurt too much."

"Jenna, don't push this. Everyone knows what you've been through. Stop now, and we can resolve this."

"No closer!"

Dee winced as the gun sight at the end of the barrel nicked into her flesh, and she saw Tyler stiffen, his hand moving toward his waist, as if his gun were still there. Then he froze, maintaining his control.

His voice lowered another half-octave. "Jenna, please listen. We can get you help—"

"I don't want your *help!* I'm just tired of the pain!" The anguished scream almost deafened Dee. With a sudden shove, Jenna launched her toward the sofa and turned the gun on Tyler. Dee screamed his name as she hit the sofa, then thudded to the floor.

The thunder of two shots reverberated off the walls, and shattered glass sprayed through the room. Dee heard herself screaming as she covered her head and felt stinging prickles dancing down her arms. As the rain of shards ended, she pushed herself off the floor, legs shaking so hard she could barely stand. Outside the window, Fletcher stood, feet braced apart, his automatic still gripped and aimed.

Dee swung around. Jenna had crumpled against the far wall, her eyes now lifeless. Tyler slumped against the front door, a patch of red growing steadily on his chest. As she clambered toward him, Dee screamed again, a sound that echoed through her mind, heart and soul.

EIGHTEEN

"You should get some rest." Maggie's warm hand gently squeezed Dee's shoulder. "Let me take you back to the hotel. Fletcher is driving the cruiser back to New Hampshire, so you could have the room. I'll watch here."

Dee lifted her head off the edge of Tyler's hospital bed, where she had drifted off a few moments before. "No, thanks. I want to be here when he wakes up."

"The docs say that could be a while."

Dee took a deep, refreshing breath, and rolled her shoulders to work out the kinks. "I know."

"But you don't care." Maggie's smile reflected her understanding.

"Would you, if it were Fletcher?"

"I'd be glued to the chair, just like you are."

"Exactly."

"But there's someone out in the hall who wants to see you." Maggie tugged on Dee's left hand. "They drove down. And I think you'll want to see them before they go back."

Puzzled, Dee followed her friend into the hall, where Jack, Nancy and Carly Bradford waited, broad smiles on their welcoming faces.

Dee's gleeful "Oh, my!" was met by a rush of small arms and legs as Carly leaped toward her with a joyful bounce. Dee knelt to grab her, and was enmeshed in a hug filled with joy and love. She kissed the top of Carly's head, relishing the sweet scent of children's shampoo blended with Carly's own aroma.

"We came to say thank you." Nancy's light words mirrored the rested, loving look on her face. "Thank you for bringing Carly back to us."

"We also came to see how Tyler is doing," Jack finished, concern on his face. "I wish I could have done the surgery, but the staff here tells me he came through with flying colors."

Dee stood, still gripping Carly's hand, and nodded. "They thought the bullet was close to his heart at first, but it turned out to be not as risky a surgery. He'll have a few weeks of recovery, but they say he's going to be okay."

Carly pulled enthusiastically on her hand. "See, I told you God would take care of us."

Dee gazed down into the bright, dark eyes that sparkled with hope and faith. "You did, indeed." She raised her head again, looking at Nancy and Jack. "Your daughter has an incredible faith. Unshakable."

Jack's grin widened. "I hope it helped. We raised her to believe, but her lack of doubt has surprised even us. For her, God simply never fails."

Carly bounced up on her tiptoes. "Well, He doesn't. My Sunday school teacher told me that we may not always like what He does or the answers He gives, but He's always there, and He always answers."

"And a little child shall lead us," murmured Maggie.

Dee took a deep breath, wishing for a moment that she had the faith of this child. She felt her heart turning toward God again, but she didn't know if she could ever have the belief in Him this glorious child did. *Maybe, someday.*

She shook Jack's hand with her free one. "Thank you for stopping by and checking on us." She reached and gave Nancy a quick hug. "I'll keep you posted on Tyler's condition."

"Can I pray for him?" Carly looked from her mother, to her father, to Dee.

Nancy shook her head. "I think you're too young to go in. We can pray for him at home."

Carly sighed and fell silent, but continued to look at both parents with pleading eyes.

Let her pray.

Dee frowned. *Where had that thought come from?* She looked at Maggie, who merely shrugged. She glanced at the nurses station, but they were all engrossed in their own business.

We should all pray.

Dee squeezed her eyes shut a moment, then looked at Nancy and Jack. "Actually," she began slowly, "if you don't mind…"

Tyler felt the pain first, the solid ache that seemed to inhabit every muscle of his body and the sharper, driving pain in his chest. Then came the awareness of voices and a faint light. Someone was talking. No… praying. A young voice.

Consciousness eased into his mind like a thick curtain being drawn back to reveal actors on a stage. Soft, warm hands gripped his own, and he could smell a light perfume above the odors of medicine and disinfectant. A scent he recognized.

Dee's perfume.

But the voice belonged to a child. "…Lord, please heal Mr. Madison and lift him up in Your love."

After a brief pause, the prayer continued, this time in a baritone that Tyler gradually realized belonged to Jack Bradford.

"Father God, this man has been faithful to You and Your Son with his life, his heart, and his mind. We ask You now to place Your healing hands on his body, heal him from these physical wounds. We know You can touch anyone with Your love."

Another silence passed, then came the voice Tyler had grown to know so well. To love.

"Lord, I know I walked away from You, but this man, this family, have shown me how great is Your love, Your care for all of us, even in the harshest of times. I hope You will forgive me, and open Your heart to this man—" Her voice faltered and she inhaled deeply "—this man I've come to love so much, and that You will heal him. All this we ask in Your Son's name. Amen."

A soft chorus of Amens followed, then the room fell silent.

Tyler swallowed, testing his throat. Sore, but maybe the words could be understood. He closed his fingers around those hands pressing against his palms and opened his eyes, squinting against the light. "You love me?" His voice was lower and raspier than he'd expected.

One hand pulled away as Carly Bradford squealed and launched herself at her dad. "I told you! See!"

Jack grabbed Carly, making low shushing noises, even as he enveloped her in a hug. She buried her face in his neck to give him a wet kiss, then twisted in his arms to look at Tyler.

Tyler tried to focus on Dee, who stood at his side, her mouth hanging partially open. Maybe she hadn't heard him…"Did you say you loved me?" he repeated.

She closed her mouth, blinking hard against a growing brightness in her eyes. She nodded, and her grip on his hand tightened almost to the point of pain.

He cleared his throat and took a deeper breath, an action that resulted in an even sharper pain in his chest. He groaned, but he had to get this out. He cleared his throat and tried again. "So you'd marry me?"

He heard gasps from behind her, and Dee lost the battle with the tears. They continued to stream down her cheeks, even though she tried to wipe them away. "Yes, I most definitely will marry you, Tyler Madison."

"Good." He closed his eyes again. "Now I have a reason to get well. I have to teach my dog to like you."

Dee giggled, then she leaned over and placed a soft kiss on his lips.

"Do that again," he whispered. And she did.

As Tyler drifted back to sleep, he sent his own prayer toward heaven. *Lord, thank You, for my life, for Carly's return, and for opening Dee's heart to Yours again. Your heart and mine.* And with that, Tyler slept with a renewed sense of purpose, peace and love.

EPILOGUE

Maggie sat on the edge of Dee's bed, watching as the hair stylist pinned the last of the baby's breath into the ringlets of Dee's hair. Satin ribbons streamed down through the curls, adding light and color to her appearance.

David, dressed in a miniature tuxedo and sitting on Maggie's lap, cooed as Dee handed him the leftover ribbons to play with. "You look gorgeous," Maggie whispered.

They were in Dee's retreat cabin, which was the only place they had found any privacy. The lodge house overflowed with the entire town of Mercer, as guests spilled out over the lawn and mingled in groups around the food. Dee's parents had arrived the day before from Tennessee, along with several of her cousins and friends, and they were the life of the party with their deep Southern accents and stories about Dee as a teenager.

Dee stood, and the hair stylist gave her hair one last fluff before gathering her tools into her bag and leaving. Dee then reached for one of Maggie's hands. "Thank you for this. I couldn't have done it without you."

"Me? I think Fletcher has found a new gift for event planning. You'd think he was holding this for his own daughter!"

Dee grinned. "I can't remember ever being this happy. Help me into the dress."

"You know it!" Maggie sat David in the middle of the bed, then helped Dee pull the long white gown from her closet. As the cloth fell free of the hanger, it brushed the emerald green dress. Mickey's dress. Dee paused, looking it over carefully for a moment.

"Maggie?"

"Yes?"

Dee pulled the green dress from her closet and handed it to Maggie. "I think this would look great on you."

Tyler felt like a stuffed sausage, and he tugged at the tight collar of his dress blues again. "Whose idea was an outdoor wedding in August?" he muttered.

Standing beside him, Fletcher chuckled. "Yours. You couldn't wait for fall, and our front lawn is the only place in Mercer big enough for all these people. You think a tuxedo is any cooler?"

Tyler looked out over the long sloping lawn that had been transformed into an alfresco chapel, complete with long sheets of white veil gracefully dancing in the trees and towers of white roses. A long white cloth ran along the ground from the front door of the lodge house to where he stood with Fletcher and the preacher. "I changed my mind. I want to honeymoon in Alaska."

"And miss introducing Miss Tennessee to Boston?"

"Well, there is—" He froze as the front door opened, and Carly and Maggie emerged. A sudden hush settled over the lawn as a guitarist began to play and sing the processional that Dee had insisted on using, an ancient folk song about timelessness of eternal love.

Carly proceeded them, tossing rose petals wildly in every direction. Maggie followed slowly, a wide, unstoppable grin on her face.

Finally, Dee's father stepped out. An elegant Southern gentleman in his late sixties, Mr. Mathis was the picture of grace as he held out his arm, and Dee stepped out to take it. Framed in white—gown, ribbons, and flowers—she shone in the bright sunlight with a golden radiance.

"Wow," Fletcher whispered.

Tyler remained silent, suddenly chilled and shaking. "I don't deserve her."

"Shut up," Fletcher said. "God sent her. Remember? Carly said so."

Tyler wasn't about to argue. As they had all discovered, the faith of Carly Bradford never failed.

* * * * *

Dear Reader,

Have you ever had something happen that made you feel overwhelmed and, quite possibly, all alone? Most of us have. Trials are a part of life, and nowhere in Scripture does God promise us a life of ease and comfort.

Instead, he promises that He'll never leave us. That He'll always help us, including putting folks in our lives who will give us the strength to climb out of the ditch. As David writes in Psalm 34:19, "Hard times may well be the plight of the righteous—they may often seem overwhelmed—but the Eternal One rescues them from them all."

When *The Taking of Carly Bradford* opens, Dee has experienced the most devastating loss any mother can. She's crushed mentally and spiritually. But God does not leave her. He sends people to help her, and, in the end, it is Dee who becomes the helper. She desperately wants to prevent another mother from going through what she has.

When God rescues us, it should never end there. As we survive and thrive, it is our turn, our time to become the rescuer that He sends forth to His children. After all, we may be the first sign of Him that some folks see.

I hope He blesses you all.

All my best,
Ramona

QUESTIONS FOR DISCUSSION

1. At the beginning of the book, what steps has Dee taken in her efforts to recover from a crushing loss?

2. How has she been helped in her efforts? Are there other steps you think she could have taken?

3. God often puts people in our lives to help us through trials. What roles have Maggie and Fletcher played in Dee's recovery?

4. How do you think Dee's friendship with Tyler has helped her find her way again?

5. Do you have people in your life who have helped you through rough times? How do you think they help you find God's plan for your life?

6. As Dee works with Tyler, she becomes determined to help the Bradfords. How have your own problems helped you see the trials others are experiencing?

7. In what way did the attacks on Dee open her mind up to God?

8. How did Tyler "plant seeds" so that Dee began to change her thoughts about God?

9. Have you had someone in your life share thoughts and beliefs that helped your faith grow and

strengthen? Have you been able to share those changes with others who might be struggling with their faith?

10. Throughout the book, Carly's faith never wavers, even when help doesn't come. Have you had times when you still relied on God, even though His help seemed delayed?

11. In the end, it's Carly's resolute faith that pushes Dee firmly back toward God. How has the faith of the children in your life affected your beliefs?

12. Jenna's mental breakdown came about because she couldn't move beyond past events. Have there been times in your life when past events kept you from moving on in life? What steps did you take to overcome this?

13. What do you think the green dress represents for Dee? Why is giving it to Maggie an important step in her relationship with Tyler?

14. *The Taking of Carly Bradford* is a story of healing and restoration. Have you seen God act in your life, or the lives of your friends and family, to bring healing from a great loss? Have you witnessed His work, even when human faith falters?

15. Is there anything in Dee's story that can inspire some part of your own life?

When her neighbor proposes a "practical" marriage, romantic Rene Mitchell throws the ring in his face. Fleeing Texas for Montana, Rene rides with trucker Clay Preston—and rescues an expectant mother stranded in a snowstorm. Clay doesn't believe in romance, but can Rene change his mind?

Turn the page for a sneak preview of
"A Dry Creek Wedding"
by Janet Tronstad,
one of the heartwarming stories
about wedded bliss in the new collection
SMALL-TOWN BRIDES.
Available in June 2009 from Love Inspired®.

"Never let your man go off by himself in a snow storm," Mandy said. The inside of the truck's cab was dark except for a small light on the ceiling. "I should have stopped my Davy."

"I doubt you could have," Rene said as she opened her left arm to hug the young woman. "Not if he thought you needed help. Here, put your head on me. You may as well stretch out as much as you can until Clay gets back."

Mandy put her head on Rene's shoulder. "He's going to marry you some day, you know."

"Who?" Rene adjusted the blankets as Mandy stretched out her legs.

"A rodeo man would make a good husband," Mandy muttered as she turned slightly and arched her back.

"Clay? He doesn't even believe in love."

Well, that got Mandy's attention, Rene thought, as the younger woman looked up at her and frowned. "Really?"

Rene nodded.

"Well, you have to have love," Mandy said firmly. "Even my Davy says he loves me. It's important."

"I know." Rene wondered how her life had ever gotten so turned around. A few days ago she thought Trace was her destiny and now she was kissing a man who would rather order up a wife from some catalogue than actually fall in love. She'd felt the kiss he'd given her more deeply than she should, too. Which meant she needed to get back on track.

"I'm going to make a list," Rene said. "Of all the things I need in a husband. That's how I'll know when I find the right one."

Mandy drew in her breath. "I can help. For you, not for me. I want my Davy."

Rene looked out the side window and saw that the light was coming back to the truck. She motioned for Mandy to sit up again. She doubted Clay had found Mandy's boyfriend. She'd have to keep the young woman distracted for a little bit longer.

Clay took his hat off before he opened the door to his truck. Then he brushed his coat before climbing inside. He didn't want to scatter snow all over the women.

"Did you see him?" Mandy asked quietly from the middle of the seat.

Clay shook his head. "I'll need to come back."

"But—" Mandy protested until another pain caught her and she drew in her breath.

"It won't take long to get you to Dry Creek," Clay said as he started his truck. "Then I can come back and look some more."

Clay didn't like leaving the man out there any more than Mandy did, but it could take hours to find him, and the sooner they got Mandy comfortable and relaxed, the sooner those labor pains of hers would go away.

"I feel a lot better," Mandy said. "If you'd just go back and look some more, I'll be fine."

Clay looked at the young woman as she bit her bottom lip. Mandy was in obvious pain regardless of what she said. "You're not fine, and there's no use pretending."

Mandy gasped, half in indignation this time.

Those pains worried him, but he assumed she must know the difference between the ones she was having and ones that signaled the baby was coming. Women went to class for that kind of thing these days. She probably just needed to lie down somewhere and put her feet up.

"He's right," Rene said as she put her hand on Mandy's stomach. "Davy wouldn't want you out here. He'll tell you that when we find him. And think of the baby."

Mandy turned to look at Rene and then looked back at Clay.

"You promise you'll come back?" Mandy asked. "Right away?"

"You have my word," Clay said as he started to back up the truck.

"That should be on your list," Mandy said as she looked up at Rene. "Number one—he needs to keep his word."

Clay wondered if the two women were still talking about the baby Mandy was having. It seemed a bit premature to worry about the little guy's character, but he was glad to see that the young woman had something to occupy her mind. Maybe she had plans for her baby to grow up to be president or something.

"I don't know," Rene muttered. "We can talk about it later."

"We've got some time," Clay said. "It'll take us fifteen minutes at least to get to Dry Creek. You may as well make your list."

Mandy shifted on the seat again. "So, you think trust is important in a husband?"

"A *husband?*" Clay almost missed the turn. "You're making a list for a husband?"

"Well, not for me," Mandy said patiently. "It's Rene's list, of course."

Clay grunted. Of course.

"He should be handsome, too," Mandy added as she stretched. "But maybe not smooth, if you know what I mean. Rugged, like a man, but nice."

Clay could feel Mandy's eyes on him.

"I don't really think I need a list," Rene said so low Clay could barely hear her.

Clay didn't know why he was so annoyed that Rene was making a list. "Just don't put Trace's name on that thing."

"I'm not going to put anyone's name on it," Rene said as she sat up straighter. "And you're the one who doesn't think people should just fall in love. I'd think you would *like* a list."

Clay had to admit she had a point. He should be in favor of a list like that; it eliminated feelings. It must be all this stress that was making him short-tempered. "If you're going to have a list, you may as well make the guy rich."

That should show he was able to join into the spirit of the thing.

"There's no need to ridicule—" Rene began.

"A good job does help," Mandy interrupted solemnly.

"Especially when you start having babies. I'm hoping the job in Idaho pays well. We need a lot of things to set up our home."

"You should make a list of what you need for your house," Clay said encouragingly. Maybe the women would talk about clocks and chairs instead of husbands. He'd seen enough of life to know there were no fairy tale endings. Not in his life.

* * * * *

Will spirited Rene Mitchell change trucker
Clay Preston's mind about love?
Find out in
SMALL-TOWN BRIDES,
the heartwarming anthology from
beloved authors Janet Tronstad and Debra Clopton.
Available in June 2009 from Love Inspired®

Love Inspired®
SUSPENSE

TITLES AVAILABLE NEXT MONTH

On sale June 9, 2009

NO ALIBI by Valerie Hansen

Jury duty was just another chore for Julie Ann Jones—until the life at stake became her own. A series of "accidents" target the jurors, and while fellow juror Smith Burnett gives Julie Ann the courage to carry on, both Julie Ann and Smith may pay the ultimate price for justice.

HER LAST CHANCE by Terri Reed
Without a Trace

Missing mother—and suspected murderer—Leah Farley is found, but with no recollection of her past. If she can't reclaim her memories, even bounty hunter Roman Black won't be able to protect her from the *real* killer, who wants to keep Leah's lost secrets buried forever.

SCENT OF MURDER by Virginia Smith

Caitlin Saylor is dazzled when she meets Chase Hollister. The candle factory owner is handsome, charming and very interested in Caitlin. But when a special gift leaves Caitlin in danger, protecting her could cost Chase his business, his reputation—or maybe his life.

BLACKMAIL by Robin Caroll

When oil rigs are sabotaged, PR representative Sadie Thompson is put on the case. Then someone threatens Sadie and Caleb, her half-brother, to make the evidence disappear. Caleb's parole officer, Jon Garrison, is watching them both closely, waiting for one of them to slip up. He doesn't trust Sadie—can she trust him? She needs Jon's help, and has nowhere else to turn.

LISCNMBPA0509